PRAISE FOR *THREE GUESSES*

"Original, eloquent, engaging, and an entertainingly memorable read from cover to cover."

—*Midwest Book Review*

"In Chris McClain Johnson's wildly entertaining and smart epistolary novella, *Three Guesses*, an unpredictable friendship is forged between three unlikely characters. When they meet, each is like a "lost character" in a story or "missing comma" in a poem, yet through their honest exchanges, they not only find each other but themselves. Frequently lyrical and rife with poems and stories, this intimate and funny book is filled with longing and heart...It will make you both plummet and rise with the love and hope strangers can and should bring to each other's lives. *Three Guesses* restores and reinforces faith in humanity."

—Deirdre Fagan, author of *Find a Place for Me*

"In a day of instant communication and surface relationships, it is refreshing to read of a deep connection that evolves through old-fashioned snail mail...the result is a testament not only to the power of words, but also to the healing prospect of genuine, authentic friendship. I didn't want it to end."

—Tracey D. Buchanan, author of *Toward the Corner of Mercy and Peace*

"This quirky wonderful book is a paean to friendship and love and creativity. I couldn't put it down. I felt uplifted on every page. For readers who loved *84 Charing Cross Road*, *Three Guesses* is a delightful successor."

—Martha Anne Toll, author of *Three Muses* and *Duet for One*

"*Three Guesses* is an absolute delight. As Sam, Richard, and Pete get to know each other through increasingly intimate letters, they open themselves up to the universe at large. Even with their faults and foibles, these characters are relatable, lovable, and so very human...I'm still smiling about this uplifting novella, which reminds us so beautifully that surprising connections can ripen between people searching for friendship."

—Heather Bell Adams, author of *Maranatha Road* and *The Good Luck Stone*

"Three strangers linked by chance through a mysterious painting forge an unlikely friendship in a years-long exchange of letters. Ghosts haunt this story—missing parents, palpable absences, destructive pasts that hover over the characters' present lives. Identities are assumed, then shed; running away becomes running toward. In *Three Guesses*, Chris McClain Johnson has crafted a novella that is a song to the groundedness and salvation that human connection provides."

—Cynthia Reeves, author of *The Last Whaler*

"Epistolary, accessible, unpredictable, and, maybe most important, charmingly readable—one way or another, Chris McClain Johnson's *Three Guesses* will make its way into your heart."

—Mark Wish, author of *Necessary Deeds*

"Chris McClain Johnson's *Three Guesses* is a big-hearted novella about three strangers who become pen pals over the chance sale of a piece of art. What begins as a lark—sending letters in the mail at the end of the twentieth century!—evolves into years of sharing loves and losses, transitions and triumphs, new homes and old ghosts. This is the story of the enduring nature of friendship, the gift of the written word, and most of all, the power of found family. *Three Guesses* is a delight!"

—Miriam Gershow, author of *Closer* and *Survival Tips: Stories*

"What a lovely story! The premise was unique, the story unfolded in a believable and very human way, and the ending was perfect."

—Willy Bearden, author of *Mississippi Hippie: A Life in 49 Pieces*

"An epistolary celebration of creativity, art, and the written word, *Three Guesses* is an enchanting treat of a novella. I absolutely adored it… Only communicating through the mail, this odd trio will come to sustain each other in the most unexpected ways. With vivid, poetic storytelling and warm humor, Chris McClain Johnson weaves their loneliness and longing into a life-affirming and joyful tapestry of connection. Warning, you might find happy tears rolling down your cheeks as you turn the last page."

—Jennifer Oko, author of *Gloss* and *Just Emilia*

"I'd planned to dip into *Three Guesses* and read just for a little bit, but the magic of the epistolary genre, that intrigue of nib-nosing into someone else's letters, was already tugging me along. The narrators, three people bound together by a chance encounter with a painting, communicate at first tersely and then with graduating levels of intimacy and openness. By the time one of them moves to Hatteras, I knew I didn't stand a chance of closing the book. Sam, Richard, and Pete's lives mirror the shifting sands of the island, swirling and dissolving, yet coming back together as a chosen family, coming back together to live on shifting sands, finally anchored."

—Heather Frese, author of *The Saddest Girl on the Beach*

"Intensely clever and often laugh-out-loud funny... Johnson's novella explores the relentless human quest for love and belonging in heartbreaking, hilarious detail, enriched by razor-sharp, often achingly beautiful prose."

—Ginger Pinholster, author of *Snakes of St. Augustine*

THREE GUESSES

Chris McClain Johnson

Regal House Publishing

Published by
Regal House Publishing, LLC
Raleigh, NC 27605
All rights reserved

ISBN -13 (paperback): 9781646036172
ISBN -13 (epub): 9781646036189
Library of Congress Control Number: 2024944624

Cover images and design by © C. B. Royal

Printed in the United States of America

Regal House Publishing, LLC
https://regalhousepublishing.com

For my heroes: Mom, Dad, and Adam

July 1998

Dear Pete Wren of New York City and Richard Mabry of Phoenix,

I'm breaking a rule or two sneaking my letter in here, but I thought you might like an introduction if you don't know each other already. The air of mystery is palpable, for me at least. Please pitch this right now if you have the slightest inkling you would turn me in. I'm giving you pause to think about it… Okay then, here's the story.

Artist Pete Wren donated his painting *Three Guesses* to the Fine Arts Donation Collective, headquartered here in Memphis, in August 1994. In short, the for-profit FADC solicits and provides high-end donations (paintings, sculptures, and such) for its non-profit members (schools, churches, and such) who in turn pay the FADC a percentage of earnings for those pieces from their fundraisers (silent auctions and such). The agency also manages all the paperwork, which is why your formal letter came from them instead of the school. I've sent along the brochure so you can puzzle your way through the program.

The catalog goes out every January and then it's a total frenzy through March as members submit their orders. There's also an underground effort to ensure high-value donations don't end up in historically mediocre events, another layer of madness. Items that don't get selected, at least not by an organization that will bring a decent profit, go into storage, some for several years. You can decide on your own if all of this is legit.

Mr. Wren's painting was not selected for the 1995 catalog, went into storage, cycled back out for this year's catalog, ended up at a private school fundraiser in Phoenix late May and sold for a whopping $6,500 to the highest bidder, Richard Mabry, who did not attend the event but had someone there in his place. This representative and his three companions, apparently quite drunk, kept bidding against each other during the live auction until the auctioneer called it in the inebriated rep's favor at four times the estimated gallery value. At that point, in a fit of drooling laughter (or so I've heard), the fellow crash-landed on the floor in front of the headmistress when the gavel was slammed down. All four of them were put into a taxi van and sent away.

Are you both aware of this tumbleweed of events? Was this planned? I can only guess that *Three Guesses* now hangs on a wall in Phoenix. Is this the case, Mr. Mabry, or do you plan to deny the bid? Do you know Pete Wren?

Reaching out to you comes from pure curiosity mixed with pure boredom on this painfully slow afternoon. I would love to hear back if you feel so inclined. Be sure to send your replies to my address, not to the FADC. I put your addresses on the back so you can include each other. I understand if you drop this right in the trash. In any case, be sure to keep the FADC letter for your tax records.

Again, I beg you not to turn me in for this. My job here is temporary for a few more weeks, so I'm not devoted to the FADC, but I do want to keep in good standing with the temp agency. I've been with them for three years now, which is no small feat.

Best regards,
SB

August 1998

Hello, SB. Richard Mabry here.

I'm sure the FADC would consider tucking your personal letter in with their business mail appallingly inappropriate and possibly criminal, especially since you shared our personal information as well. In addition, not providing your full name was rather sophomoric since one phone call to them with your address would quickly reveal your identity. Meanwhile, why date your letter with only the month and year? This is yet another sliver of vague, but since you consider the actual day unimportant, I've followed along.

As for the story you recounted, I do know some of the details but do not intend to challenge the bid. How can I? It wasn't the school's fault. The representative was my partner, my 'former' partner as of last week. On the night of this debacle, we were having another heated argument about money, specifically about how much of mine he was spending, when his carload of crazies pulled up and pried him off to a restaurant opening. How did they end up at a private school fundraiser? I have no idea and honestly don't care. The whole bloody thing saved me more in the long run than the cost of the painting, I assure you. So, no, this was not planned. I don't know Pete Wren and appreciate the introduction since his intriguing work of art is now hanging in my world. I will not be turning you in. Hopefully he won't either.

Three Guesses is exquisite and mysterious, like a soft poem surrounded by a bold storm. It's simply mesmerizing, forever changing with the lights and darks of day and night, shadows from the textures growing deep and stretched by late afternoon. I love it. Please do tell us about it, Mr. Wren, and what it represents. I've enclosed a picture in case you need a jog.

Sincerely,
Richard Mabry

August 1998

To SD and Richard Mabry,

I don't have time for this crap, so of course I'm not turning anyone in. I might have been interested but find it ridiculous SB signed off with initials. It pains me to even write SB. I hate initials and chopped names, except with my agent Julz since Julz is elegant while Julie is dull and overused. Julz is more of a nickname than a slice, nowhere near basement-level chopping like SB.

Have nice lives, you kooks.
Leave me alone.
Pete Wren

February 1999

Dear SB and Pete Wren,

I was tempted to write again last year, then the holidays took over, then I found Pete Wren's nasty reply buried in my junk drawer this morning. My curiosity was again piqued. I wonder: Why respond at all if you don't have time for such crap? And why tell us to have nice lives? All that effort to write, copy, and mail your tiny letter took more than a quick minute, quite a lot of work to expend on a couple of kooks. I don't believe you want to be left alone, Mr. Wren. I believe you've been waiting to hear back from us. So, here *I* am at least.

I'm most surprised we haven't heard back from the perpetrator of this potential correspondence crime. Where are you, SB? Since neither of us turned you in, at least tell us your real name or we'll be forced to make one up. Imagine where our imaginations might go with those initials.

I have little to share except I have a new partner, James, who moved in with me rather quickly and who appears to adore me but absolutely does not like *Three Guesses*. It's not realistic enough for him, but I refuse to put it out of sight. I love it more every day and hoped we might hear a bit about it instead of barbs.

I expect a word in return from you both since I've

made the effort yet again to connect. While waiting for your replies, I'm going to pretend it's summer and have my near-famous Popping Paloma. Try it. I promise you'll like it.

Richard's Popping Paloma

Ice cubes
2 ounces blanco tequila
2 ounces fresh grapefruit juice
1 tablespoon agave nectar or simple syrup
2-3 ounces club soda
Fresh lime

Rim a cocktail glass with a lime wedge then dip it in salt. Add ice, tequila, juice, and syrup. Top it off with soda and a good squeeze of lime juice then give this fizzy fav a gentle stir. Voila! Suddenly it's July!

Back in touch and possibly back in love,
Richard

March 1999

Hello, Richard and Pete,

So glad to hear from you again, Richard! Thanks so much for your persistence, and please accept my apology for signing off with initials. My name is Sam Brooks. I wasn't comfortable sending my name the first time, but you're absolutely right. I'm easy to trace.

I can't stand my given name Sherry, not the name itself but as a name for me in particular. It doesn't fit me. And no hating on Sam, Pete, because it's not chopped from Samantha. It was my dad's grandfather's name. Sam Brooks. Not Samuel or Samson, only Sam. He didn't even have a middle name. When I decided to switch to Sam the day I turned eighteen, Dad said it was fitting and that I'm just like my great-grandfather—unsettled, a bona fide rambler—the complete opposite of Dad, who plans everything to a pencil-pointed period and lives firmly inside his mid-life routine. I'm sure they struggled to get along. Probably Granddaddy Sam and I would have been peas in a pod, but he died before I could walk.

Anyway, I blew off this idea of connecting when we got Pete's snarky response. It didn't seem worth pursuing anymore. Plus, I've been playing with an old relationship that got rekindled and we moved in together, again. So my focus shifted, again. His name is Neal. I'm remembering all the reasons we broke up the first time. I'm struggling with him on so many levels, I can't even. It's a novel. I doubt we'll make it to the next chapter.

It's early spring here in the south. 'Tis the season that pinches my craving for change. It also inspires me to get off my duff after a long winter's night and start back with my walking routine (which lasts only until the summer heat swoops in), so think of me if you hear "Walking in Memphis" on the radio. Note that my feet will be five feet off Peabody in midtown instead of ten feet off of Beale downtown.

Thanks to you both for not turning me in! I moved on from the FADC months ago but still work for the temp agency. They keep me hopping all over the city week to week, which is a good thing since I'm not good at staying planted at one job or with one person for long. Can you tell I'm easily bored? I have the attention span of a housefly caught in a lampshade.

But this is fun, right? I love sending real letters, and I really love getting them in the mail. Please don't go away, Pete. We're not kooks. Let's plunge right in and be grown-up pen pals. It will be a little adventure. And we can use email if you have it, but only if we all agree. We don't ever have to talk or meet in person. It would be nice, though, to know more about you—what you're like, what you look like, what your voices sound like.

As for me, I won't be making any fancy magazine covers. Hair: long, brown and wavy. I play with braids and knots and clips and headbands, so it looks different every day. Eyes: brown with stubby eyelashes. Build: average at five foot seven, lingering around 135 pounds. Voice: a little on the deep end like my dad's and a bit raspy like Stevie Nicks. I love her songs and every kind of music except head-banging thrashers and over-the-top sopranos. I'm pretty introverted and a bit bohemian (I dress like a total hippie when not at work) and regularly ponder the purpose and source of our souls.

Hope you'll share too! Happy spring!

Your grown-up pen pal,
Sam Brooks

PS: I got all the fixings, Richard, and will be making your Popping Paloma this weekend!

May 1999

Dear Sam Brooks and Richard Mabry,

Yesterday someone pushed a woman out of a window. She fell nine stories. I've been waiting for something interesting to happen before getting back to you kooks. The news reporter said she had suffered brain trauma from a massive blow to the head before hitting the ground, bludgeoned by her pusher. Like we need to know this.

I stayed up all night painting her plunging past a grungy apartment building. She had to look as if she was falling, even the hair on her arms straight up from the wind. I couldn't make her face, so you see her from the side with hair and limbs flailing. I named it *Without Warning*. It's the least abstract thing I've done in years. Julz, my one true friend (and more) and highly successful gallery owner, is setting up a show for me in a few months. I may make the whole thing about people falling. Seems appropriate for New York City, or for humanity in general. We're all falling all the time. Some of us are lucky enough to have someone or something to catch us before we hit the ground, even if it's a change in perspective, or even a change in the weather.

A couple of years ago, a woman came to the studio for a look at a painting called *Wondering Ju*. She seemed shy, so Julz left her alone and called me down to see if I recognized her. I did. She'd been at the opening the night before with an obnoxious group. One of the idiots spit on me while proclaiming my work was "bent on a balance." What does that mean? Maybe he was confusing me with the sculptor in the gallery next door. Whatever. I remembered her because she was the only quiet one in the group. And because she was beautiful.

Wondering Ju is a real crowd pleaser, dusty with the outline of a woman barely visible walking along a waterline barely visible. Our visitor sat down on the bench and stared at it for a long time, tracing the outline of her neck and shoulders with her fingers. I watched her from the back steps and got so ramped up that I fell and knocked over a stack of glass shelves that crashed into a million pieces. She looked back at me with a pained expression then flew out the door. I'll never forget her glare, like I'd taken something precious from her. I've imagined many different lives for her. I've imagined my free and easy *Ju* giving her some piece, or peace, of passion she yearned for. She shows up in my sketches sometimes. I think she might be my falling woman.

A man came in later that day and bought *Wondering Ju* right off the wall. Julz was distant all afternoon and didn't speak to me or even look at me when I was cleaning up the glass mess. I was crushed. I painted it for her and couldn't believe she let someone walk away with it. What if I left for good? This was her question.

She would be left with this *Ju* on her wall like a tribute to something lost. This was her reasoning.

I did leave soon after that. I miss living with her, but we're better apart. She's not as possessive. It's odd she wants it this way, not able to keep her eyes on me all the time. You can't be jealous of what you can't see. She explores too. Fine with me, but she would be furious to know how many women have been in and out of here.

I love women. I crave the erotic essence of women, their lines, their depths, the softness in their faces that separate them from men. There are no ugly women, not really. Julz argues that her assistant Chele is horrifying. Chele is chopped from Michele, of course, and I admit she is hard to look at, skinny as straw with yellowy skin and ill-patterned features all around, but she has an inward beauty. For someone so stark, she is soft and humble. She loves my paintings, traces every stroke with her bulging eyes. Like the woman with *Wondering Ju*, Chele is deeply stirred by my work.

I'm rambling. It's unusually hot here for May, and I haven't slept well in days. I'm telling you all of this I guess as an olive branch for being such a jerk before, my attempt at being a pen pal, but I'm not going to describe myself except to say that very, very loud music of all kinds fuels my artistic spirit. And yes, some songs are crazy dark and chaotic.

Thanks for sharing your real name, Sam Brooks. Otherwise, you wouldn't have heard from me again.

And I appreciate your love of *Three Guesses*, Richard Mabry. Now change the tide, please, and tell us more of love.

Without warning,
Pete

August 1999

Hello, Pen Pals! My apologies for taking so long to rejoin the buzz.

Sam Brooks, I'm a fan of your actual name and its history. While SB certainly could have been your nickname (for instance, I know a TJ and an AB), that kind of chop didn't seem to fit.

Pete Wren, how exciting you've hopped into this adventure. Please do tell us, and hopefully this is not a sore request, if Pete is chopped from Peter. Since sliced and diced names irritate you, I can't imagine you would do the same to yours, so please clear that up for us.

There's so much going on here and no less than three birthday soirees this weekend, all of which I would love to skip. By the way, happy birthdays whenever they are. Mine is coming up in September. The date and year are inconsequential, though I will tell you I'm a Libra, and I'm pretty spot on with the characteristics put forth by one Druzella the Seer who confirmed them while reading my fortune some years ago in New Orleans. What she predicted at the time never turned up, but the astrological personality was spot on. I'm a charming people pleaser and not as much of a social butterfly as my celestial counterparts. I'm happy pleasing at home. I'll leave it there.

What do I look like? I've never had to describe

myself before but basically tall and lanky with the beginnings of a receding hair line, thin eyebrows, glasses, tenor-like voice. I don't have any particular visual quality that makes me stand out in a crowd. I simply melt in, though I do wear fabulous hats and bright shirts sometimes that might draw attention. I love being with friends, very few family members, and lovers (well, sometimes) as much as I enjoy being alone. I'm a jazz kind of guy at home but secretly rock out to the day's Top 40 in my car. I've been in research more years than I can count in a variety of fields that might bore you. I have an intense kinship with the library and read at least four books a week, and I'm currently transitioning to a mostly Mediterranean diet to curb my cholesterol.

Enough about me, and enough about heat, Pete! You know nothing of it like we do here in Phoenix in August. But I will indulge you and say something of love. I have concluded, after listening to my assistant Paulette rant and rave over the last few months, that people do change when they get married, and not because they are suddenly married but because marriage suddenly gives birth to a huge storm of expectations.

You see, people try to blame relational upset on the universal ones: she'll lose weight, we'll have sex every night, he'll pick up after himself, we'll start a family. But the unexpected ones are the clues to marital de-bliss. For instance, Paulette never expected her new groom to side with his mother on their many important decisions. She never expected him to solicit the MIL's opinion in the first place, but now he runs to her for everything, even what colors to paint their walls. This is turning everything upside down for my dear friend. She feels deceived. I warned her to just live with this fellow, nothing more, but she poured concrete.

I can relate. James is changing too. Without warning! It's perplexing. You think you know someone or know what drives them your way, but he seems to be driving in the opposite direction of late. Maybe it's work. Maybe it's something else. Maybe it's someone else. He's an Aries: ambitious, opinionated, a bit (or more) arrogant, resolute. I'm shillyshally, indecisive. Vacillating comes to mind. I dither and dawdle and craftily avoid conflict.

We're hosting one of the birthdays as a dinner party Saturday night. James is trying on his culinary skills with an Indian spread. I'll be interested to see him get that right. I will definitely be looking for signs with our guests, pathetic as it sounds, but something is off with him. He should be careful. Get a little wine in me and I might try on some conflict, see how it looks with my new dinner jacket.

Is love in the air?
Richard

September 1999

Hey, guys!

Hope you both survived the summer heat. I have no idea about New York temps for you, Pete, but I know Richard gets that dry desert heat. Down here in Memphis, we get relentless humidity so thick it's hard to breathe. Even near the end of September we're barely getting relief.

Happy belated birthday, Richard! Mine was late August. Virgo. But I think I'm more in line with you Libras. All I know is I'm now having a total anxiety attack about turning thirty next year. I didn't write sooner because this is all I've had on my mind. I'm officially moving toward old-maidism, and all that comes with this fact and fear has consumed me.

Will I ever get married? I'm not sure I'm a tie-the-knot sort of person. And if it's true that women who haven't married by the time they're forty have a greater chance of being killed in a terrorist attack than getting hitched, I guess I'll be gunned down in the street at some point in the next decade. Or the world will indeed explode as some predict when we turn 2000 in a minute, and I won't have to worry about age and love and marriage anymore. Still, it would be nice to go down with someone at my side. At least it won't be that putz Neal. I kicked him out. Again.

I'm headed out to an interview this afternoon for something more permanent, my third this week and a tough decision as you know since I can't stay settled in the same place too long before boredom or claustrophobia sets in. You would think temporary gigs help solve this malady, but they're wearing on me. I've been in six offices over the last two months. You have to be quick and stay on your toes with this kind of work. Sometimes it's stressful. Other times I struggle to keep my brain functioning.

Last week I spent one whole hour in a tiny closet shredding documents. What a great use of my higher education! I came up with a song to keep from falling asleep. It's basically The Blues: Sittin' here by myself, feel like a clock ticking on a shelf, got no view to anyone else, just ripping up paper...

I wish I had exciting news to share instead of my age-mania stress, but nada, nothing. Next time I'll come up with something more interesting, even if it's about someone else.

Songwriter Sam

November 1999

Sam and Richard,

Little bits and pieces of your faces dance around on the black canvas in my head. I imagine Richard's right eye falling off the upper left corner with a light gray lash to keep it from melting into the dark. I pull a thin silver circle from the dent below the half eye to hint at spectacles. Sam, your lips sit in the middle with a slight white line below to scar your chin. Light from the window holds its ray steady on the slender eyebrow I imagine on your forehead. I wonder how you might cock it, how it moves when you blink, how quiet and still it lays on your skin while you sleep.

Since *Without Warning* everything has turned. It's nearly ruined my life. Everything is so dark and detailed, strangely detailed like messages you get in dreams that disappear the second you wake up. I go through these phases, wondering why I paint, why I can't do anything else but paint and dream and eat bad takeout food, why sometimes I can't paint at all. At all!

Two friends from Boston showed up. They've been here three weeks. I can't get rid of them. They said they were coming through for a few days, but I can't get them out and I can't paint while they're here. As if they understand anything, they critique me. I feel kidnapped and paint canvases only in my mind and dreams.

Since childhood, I've had this recurring dream of getting lost in a crowd and separated from my sister Colly (short for Colleen, which is my fault because I couldn't say the 'een' part when I was little). She was the only reason I survived childhood. One of the worst times my father threw my mom across the room, Colly got right up in his hard sweaty drunk face and told him, "You'll pass out in a little while, but I won't and Mama won't and Petey won't. We're three times hate, Daddy, so together we're three times stronger than you." She was nine. She was brave. I can't believe he didn't punch her lights out.

In the dream, Colly fades away in the drumming roar of loud music, and I get pushed into an alley. There's an old toothless man there. He waves at me to watch out for a gang of boys. They want my shoes. This is the dream over and over and over. I want to paint it, hoping that will release it. But I can't. I can't paint anything. All I get is a wash of grays and blacks, and I hate it because I want something sane to come of it.

This is getting more depressing by the word, so I'll leave you with a little poem I wrote this morning. Consider it your Christmas present, although I despise Christmas.

Also, an ugly kitten has taken up residence here. He's a wiry critter with eyes too big for his head. I call him Jamber. He might be the only thing keeping me sane, if that's even possible.

Yours in shadow,

Pete (not Peter and certainly not Petey, except for Colly long ago)

The world is my shadow
of long-past lives
colored with harmony
not so perfect
as a well-fingered chord
on a finely tuned piano

January 2000

Happy 21st century! We're alive! We didn't explode!

Richard, did you get everything sorted out with James?

Pete, I loved your poem. Do you remember any of those lives?

I'm reading *There Is a River* about the psychic Edgar Cayce whose philosophy was that we keep coming back until we are no longer confined by flesh. This is when we can return to our original purpose. Otherwise, we spin on the merry-go-round of reincarnation.

He proposed that in the beginning was a sea of spirit. Static, content, aware, contemplative. Then it moved, became restless, desired to express itself, desired companionship. This was God and God's first thought, then came the cosmos and all the souls in it, all the companions all at once. None before and none since.

Is this it then—the true birth of our souls? Is this what we are—companions for God?

Cayce says the soul has two states of consciousness: one of spirit with knowledge of its identity and one of identity with knowledge of its experiences. The soul is given free will and is expected to go through an unlimited cycle of experience that completes when it remembers its true identity with God (which a soul tends to forget with all that freedom) and eventually merges back with spirit, returning to its source as the companion it was meant to be. Maybe he was channeling Rumi, who said, "My soul is from elsewhere, I'm sure of that, and I intend to end up there."

It all sounds a bit crazy, but somehow it makes sense to me. Individual entities, the souls of you and me, are out of control with our own free will, going around and around on the experience carousel and in the process whirling further and further from our original purpose. I wonder if that's why there are so many people now. So many souls are so far gone they keep circling here instead of heading back toward this so-called companionship. I wonder how many lifetimes I've had and if I will ever make my way back to God, back to the original elsewhere. It seems like a lofty goal.

Here's another headful. Cayce says a soul picks a particular human body and even has a plan for the experience ahead. The soul might occupy a body months before birth or even wait a while after, hovering around until it decides whether or not to take hold. And even then, it may not stay.

Seriously? What a twisted swizzle stick for the brain and something I never would have dreamed up on my own. I try to imagine myself as a vague shimmer of light hovering over my mom's belly, me in my pure form of soul deciding if I should join her journey. If that's how it works, if my soul chose my body and her for a mother, I can't figure out why. She certainly didn't stick around long.

Someone once told me they believe whole families make arrangements to meet in future lifetimes. I've tried to imagine sitting in front of a cozy fire with my parents in some long-ago era laying out our plans of reunion. Why exactly did we pick this lousy setup? My life has been such nothing for so many years, maybe always. No direction. No ambition. No mother. Maybe her selfish decision is the core reason for the absence of direction and ambition. Or maybe this lack of vision is inherited from my chosen namesake, the other rambling Sam Brooks.

I saw a woman smack her kid in the grocery this morning because he was tailing her with an orange. "That ain't on our list!" she screamed. He was maybe four. I wanted to knock her out cold and take him away to somewhere safe, thinking his soul picked wrong and his family reunion plans got waylaid like mine. But nowhere seems totally safe. Everywhere is filled with questionable souls far, far away from their original purpose.

All these things are signs, don't you think? I've decided lately everything is a sign. Something of an ice storm hit here last night and knocked out the power, so I sat on the floor in the den layered with blankets and surrounded by candles. It felt tribal. Primal. I listened for some profound message from my inner self, from my past selves, from my soul calling on me to consider the roots of my existence, my true origin, my identity, my purpose. But the only sound was silence and an occasional siren. My breath froze in midair. Shadows surrounded me. They were my own shadows of who I've been, who I'm supposed to be or will become. Hokey, right? I imagine you get it, Pete. A brush with shadowland.

Did we all formulate a plan in some other life to come together in this one? Are we supposed to meet in person or will we only send letters for eternity? Maybe our initial decision will never change, but it sure feels like everything else is changing in some undersided way. I know for sure I've got to get out of here. I don't know where to, but it's got to happen soon.

Christmas sucked again. Alone again, naturally, except I did spend about an hour with Dad. It was weird. Nothing new about that. We don't know how to be together or what to talk about. He spends a lot of time with his friend Colton who got divorced last year. He's even invited him to come stay at the house and asked if I mind giving up my room, so I've got to clean out what's left because his buddy is indeed moving in. My apartment is tiny, so I'll have to box up whatever I want to keep, which isn't much, and put it in the attic.

I'm glad he's got the company. I sure haven't been much of that for him since my mom jettisoned from life here on earth. Maybe she's back to being God's pal, but I doubt it. I doubt God wants people like her back.

Anyway, all I know is I want to be somewhere lazy and peaceful where I can be thoughtful on a different level, meet different people, eat different food, see different things, feel altogether different. I might even come to your corners of the world if you'll allow it, but we all have to agree. In the meantime, send your letters to the new return address in case I take off like tomorrow. It's Dad's, and his address will never change. I'll let you know where I end up when I get there.

Lost old soul,
Sam

March 2000

Dearest Sam and Pete,

Apologies again for the long gap in my correspondence!

Interesting reverie from you two, I must say. Sam, you depress and intrigue me at the same time. Running free for a while sounds riveting, but please don't come to my corner of the world. I rather like us not knowing each other in person. Our letters and my visions of you both are quite exquisite and profound. Don't go to Pete either, because then you two would have something without me, and our mail-only pact would be broken. Let's keep it this way always, our strange little clandestine camaraderie. Some mysteries aren't meant to be solved. Maybe that was our intention in the distant past when we were making plans to reunite here. Maybe *Three Guesses* has more meaning than Pete intended.

Speaking of mysteries, James has made a significant turn. I believe things were off with him the last time I wrote. It stayed that way for a while and contributed to my fade-out in writing. It's unsettling, especially with such a dramatic backstroke. I got home from work early last week to find him all whirled up in a reawakened debut of affection and charm. We had reached that point of hardly standing the smell of each other. Then, like flipping a light switch, we fell right back in. Tomorrow I start therapy, not only for this relationship drama but for everything. Can you believe I've stooped to this? A shrink! A nephew of a friend of my cousin's is going to prod my psyche. Maybe I'll find some past life that explains my present situation. Mysteries extraordinaire!

For Christmas, I went to see Mother in Doras, California (where, God bless me, I was forced to grow up) and spent as much time as the weather would allow in her stunning backyard. The front yard is plain with a few bushes against the house while the back is a botanist's paradise, a museum of flowers and shrubs and vines. Around the side of the house is her watering station. All she has to do is lift a big metal handle and water spews out of dozens of tiny holes she's punctured in her hose maze with an old-fashioned ice pick.

Two hundred and fifty feet of green rubber tubing snakes around things most people could never identify. And all stolen! I don't think Mother has legally acquired a single plant in her life. She takes them from her neighbors and seems to have one of every kind of thing that will grow there. Poppies, six kinds of violet, three kinds of clover, wild licorice, spearmint, peppermint, hawkweed, Jerusalem artichoke, and something she calls a one-sided pyrola. Don't think I know what I'm talking about. This is a minor list of the native ones. I can't pronounce let alone spell the others.

As usual, she walked me around pointing and naming her victims. I hope, hope, and hope I never have to take a polygraph. Truly, I wish she wouldn't tell me who is missing their loot.

I stayed through New Year's, the equivalent of thirty years in Doras time. I guess she told people her son is gay since my last visit. Either that or they've always known, or it's simply becoming more obvious as the world at large wavers in its acceptance of us. There seems to be a trend in their thinking there, that a man sitting cross-legged and alone with his mother is gay without question. People behave differently the moment this perception is public.

You think California and you think new school, forward thinking, but not in Doras. Those people live in a different era. Women pitch their voices up, along with their eyebrows, as they casually slap your arm like they would a female friend, like they have the right because their confidence in their feminine identity gives them the right. Men, straight men mind you, barely look at you for several reasons. One, they are outrageously disgusted. Two, they are outrageously confused. Three, the very notion of being with another man stirs up outrageous discomfort, and we can't have that now, can we?

IT'S OKAY. I'M GAY. This is a button I wanted to have on in the Dulver House dining room. Or reverse: I'M GAY. IT'S OKAY. Two totally different meanings for two totally different mindsets. The latter seems more appropriate for Doras. An affirmation for distinction, which never served me growing up there and why I left seconds after my high school graduation. My car had been packed for days. I threw my cap in the air, hugged Mother, zoomed away, and arrived hours later at my cousin's house here in Phoenix. He helped me get set up at Arizona State University, and his dear wife agreed to let me live with them rent-free the entire four years I was an ASU Sun Devil. Then I moved maybe six times in ten years before buying this condo with my 'at the time' cheating partner. We had such a ghastly break-up he didn't even make me buy out his half, crammed what little he had into a U-Haul and squealed away. I'm forever grateful I never introduced him to Mother.

She didn't know what to think when I first unlocked the closet moons ago. I had it deadbolted with her for the longest time. I didn't come out all at once, cracked the door open enough for her to peek in. She didn't understand. Then I started bringing my best friend Bill along on visits and we talked with her about it. The hardest thing was convincing her we weren't lovers (or 'intimates' as she called us), that we were friends like she is friends with her neighbor Elsa, no intimacy involved.

This is a difficult concept for a woman who's lived in a small town all her life, a woman so sheltered she's never heard of sushi and still has a rotary dial phone. To crisscross friendship and companionship and love and intercourse within one gender is a bit overwhelming for someone born at the start of World War I, someone who's never ventured a hundred miles from home. She was almost forty when she had me, which was terrifically risky back then and could probably explain some of my quirks and hers.

It was a rainy Tuesday evening when she stopped trying to figure it out and accepted Bill and me for what we are. Or were. Of all things, Bill died of AIDS. Cliché, right? He spent his last days with her in Doras. She cared for him like a second son. People talked. They walked by her house and pointed. Some sick freak was inside, they decided. Ha! When he was feeling good, he took her shopping. I can still imagine them poking around other people's yards on a moonless night dig-dig-digging then snip-snip-snipping to make things look old and settled.

I didn't mean for this to be so novelesque. I'm sure I'll get things worked out. Life is one phase after another, right? It could be another button.

Phased out,
Richard

Well, one last thing on the subject of soul. Despite perceptions and philosophies, there is still something tangible to life. Desoxyribonucleic Acid. DNA. The double helix. The one tangible thing that keeps us individual. As observed by Gustav Eckstein, it keeps us jailed while it keeps on making exact copies of itself—keeping you, you and me, me.

Meanwhile, eighteenth-century poet Marie-Francois-Xavier Bichat defined life as the sum of the forces that resist death. I wonder if it is resisting death or simply resisting the movement to another consciousness, or maybe in the end resisting the God-companion it was meant to be. I've no doubt that I am an old soul with countless past lives. I've certainly been on this carousel more than once. I'm curious to know if we carry the same DNA on all these rides. Surely we do. An entire field of research could be created to match us up with our past selves. Ideal proof of reincarnation!

Oh, one other thing, and I throw this in simply for amusement—the ever-evolving "Live from Richardnation" list. Packaged up, these -ation words (plus twice as many more scribbled in notebooks and lodged in my noggin) might define the whole of life, and there seems to be no end to them. Send any that are missing and I'll get them added. Maybe I'll make a poster for easy reference! Be clear. They must be four syllables only. Anticipation won't fly.

Consider yourself warned. This quickly becomes an obsession. You'll start hearing -ation words you never knew existed. You'll start seeing one in every paragraph, and I promise you'll race to see if it's already made the list. You'll come across five- and six-syllable

-ation words that will throw you into a fit of angst because they simply don't fit the rule. I tried to start those lists, and they petered out long ago.

My final note: I forgot to tell you last time I rescued a cat, a pathetic thing and nothing special to look at but the sweetest little critter in the world. I call him Jax, like a brother to Pete's Jamber. James is allergic, ha! James, Jamber, Jax. We have a trend here!

LIVE from RICHARDNATION

abdication
aberration
acclimation
accusation
activation
adaptation
admiration
adoration
advocation
affectation
affirmation
aggravation
aggregation
allegation
allocation
alteration
altercation
ambulation
amputation
animation
annexation
annotation
application

arbitration
aspiration
augmentation
aviation
avocation
bilocation
calculation
calibration
cancellation
captivation
carbonation
celebration
circulation
coloration
combination
commendation
compensation
compilation
complication
computation
concentration
condemnation
condensation

confirmation
confiscation
confrontation
conjugation
connotation
consecration
conservation
consolation
constellation
consultation
consummation
conversation
convocation
copulation
coronation
corporation
correlation
culmination
cultivation
decimation
declaration
declination
decoration
dedication
defamation
defecation
deformation
dehydration
delegation

demonstration
deportation
deprecation
deprivation
derivation
desecration
designation
desolation
desperation
destination
devastation
deviation
disclamation
dislocation
dissertation
distillation
divination
domination
duplication
education
elevation
elongation
emigration
emulation
escalation
estimation
evocation
exaltation
excavation

exclamation	illustration
expectation	imitation
expiration	immigration
explanation	implantation
exploitation	implication
exploration	importation
exportation	incantation
exultation	incarnation
fabrication	inclination
fascination	incubation
federation	indentation
fermentation	indication
figuration	indignation
fluctuation	infestation
formulation	infiltration
fornication	inflammation
fumigation	information
generation	inhalation
germination	innovation
gradiation	inspiration
graduation	installation
granulation	instigation
gravitation	insulation
habitation	integration
herniation	intimation
hesitation	intonation
hibernation	invitation
hyphenation	invocation
ideation	irrigation

irritation
isolation
iteration
jubilation
juvenation
laceration
lamination
legislation
levitation
liberation
limitation
liquidation
litigation
lubrication
lumination
marination
mastication
masturbation
maturation
mediation
medication
meditation
menstruation
mitigation
moderation
molestation
motivation
navigation
nomination

obligation
observation
occupation
operation
ovulation
pagination
palpitation
penetration
perforation
permeation
permutation
perspiration
pigmentation
pollination
population
preparation
presentation
preservation
proclamation
procreation
propagation
provocation
publication
quantization
radiation
realization
recitation
reclamation
recreation

reformation
registration
regulation
relaxation
relocation
renovation
replication
reputation
reservation
respiration
restoration
revelation
salivation
salutation
sanitation
saturation
scintillation
segmentation
segregation
separation
simulation
situation
speculation
stimulation
stipulation
strangulation
sublimation
subluxation
supplication

syndication
tabulation
termination
titillation
toleration
transformation
transportation
trepidation
tribulation
triplication
ulceration
urination
vaccination
vacillation
validation
valuation
variation
vegetation
ventilation
vindication
violation
visitation

April 2000

Sam,

I agree with Richard. Don't come to my corner either if you're out wandering around, especially if you're still roaming about on Memorial Day or July 4th, the next memorials we get to endure with all the hoopla. NYC craves hoopla and makes cake of every holiday, even though the histories behind these two include trails of death and destruction and darkness.

Everything to me seems dark right now. My painting is dark. My life is dark in general. A phase, right? Sounds like a disease. I need a button too. BEWARE! I'M IN A PLAGUE PHASE. Movie title: PHASE of the PLAGUE. Maybe truth: LOST ARTIST.

I'm thinking of somewhere I can squeeze sand between my fingers and toes, see the horizon, fall asleep with the whoosh of the surf. I could set up a stand on a boardwalk and paint fat men in floral shirts and sun-weathered women in…well, in nothing I suppose. I don't know. NYC might miss my bend on a balance, but it certainly wouldn't miss this story I wrote forever ago. I found it inside an old portfolio when I was cleaning up after the Boston buttheads. I can't tell you when I wrote it or why, but it seems fitting with all this talk of souls and shadows.

Richard, I'm shocked you're missing constipation.

Constipated,
Pete

"Shadows on the Moon"
by Pete Wren

I come from a place where sister ghosts live, shadowy divas of sea and sound dancing on the night waves under new moons and old moons and moons in between, twirling across the deep where distant shiplights haunt the foggy air. From the front porch, I watched them traveling back and forth, telling their own what they had learned. Chaos for those of us caught in between.

Storytellers say that one Sunday at twilight the older sister Leandra rowed out into the sound and fell asleep. A storm came up and pushed her crooked little boat through the channel toward the sea. As was customary on Sundays, everyone ate a tremendous breakfast then slept from early afternoon to early Monday morning, so no one saw her leave, not even her little sister Lanella, who was nestled down deep in her own Sunday sleep.

The next morning, Lanella awoke to find her sister's bed empty and unmade, which thrilled her because Leandra followed all rules to the point of boredom while Lanella was continuously in trouble for breaking them. She skipped down the stairs, the smell of sizzled bacon hanging thick in the air, to find only her mother at the table writing a letter. Her father and brother were on their way out for the day's catch, drenched grass beneath their boots.

Leandra's purple scarf was found snagged on the jetty. Horns were blown. The village came running. Lanella raced out across the rocks, despite the raging screams to come back, and reached out for the scarf right when a gull came by and snatched it away. She fell hard and broke her skull wide open.

People claimed they heard Leandra's cries in the wind and saw the gull soaring over the village with the scarf hanging from its mouth. Fishermen swore they saw it still on the jetty, flapping wildly like a pennant, Leandra's haunt reminding them they hadn't come for her. Over time they ignored the sightings and wails until the sisters were forgotten altogether. This angered Leandra so desperately she returned to tell past generations what lazy children they'd borne. Lanella countered the claims and warned the future of her sister's lies. And so began their dance, their haunting of the past, present, and midnights to come.

I believed the scarf was meant for me, that it would come to me tattered and soiled, and I would mend it like new. Then the ghost sisters could rest peacefully in death.

This is how I came to be here, sitting on a different, gray-skied spit of land hidden away from the world to calm my lunacy. My parents think I'm tainted. I was ten when they brought me here. They tell me tomorrow is the last day of my twenties and not to expect a visit.

I wouldn't be here at all if Doc hadn't found me. I would be dead. He owned an old sharpie he named *The Milwaukee*. He called her *Milly* for short and took people out on sound rides. Fancy people with fancy shoes. They can fancy themselves all over my boat, he'd say, as long as they bring plenty of fancy bills. He patted the men's backs and kissed the women's hands.

Me and *Milly* got a special relationship, he told me. She was his sanctuary, that old boat. His lover. His dreamer. His pretend friend carrying him off day after day.

My own pretends certainly carried me off. One night, I saw Leandra's scarf riding the twilight breeze near the shore. I moved slowly across the dunes and into the water to reach for it. The waves tickled my feet. The breeze kissed my face. Then a gull flew over and snatched it. I fell and found myself swept up by the waves and carried so far out I couldn't see the harbor lights. I didn't know which way to swim, so I gave in and let the sea take me.

Doc started searching for me early the next morning, before anyone else knew I was missing, and found me on the jagged rocks of the jetty, right where Lanella cracked open her skull. I was in a coma for three weeks. Doc was there when I woke up. He said I have a gift and don't know what to do with it. He promised to tell me more but never got the chance. This was the episode of my undoing. My parents swooped me up the second I was released and brought me here where there are no sea ghosts dancing and telling tales.

There are different ghosts here. Lydia, the gypsy of my veins, my soul's ghost, surfaced here. She claimed that like my own, fates can change. Like in music when one finger lingers a little too long over the F, for instance, the piece changes somehow. It may sound perfectly harmonic the rest of the way through, but something changed, and that something will surface perhaps years or lifetimes down the road. Lydia said it was simple and smooth and past time the way life happens. She said I would understand someday, and I think I do now.

I think Martin came from the lingering over a key, come simply from a hesitant note. He was real, but not real at all. He, too, was a soul's ghost, out to captivate me for a moment so he could capture Lydia for a lifetime. She knew this, I'm sure. She knew he was coming for her.

I was sitting on the porch daydreaming. It was spring. I remember because there were daffodils everywhere and a mockingbird in the mulberry squawking over the train rumbling in the distance. I sat there with my eyes closed wishing I was on that train riding hobo in an empty car with my feet hanging out of the open doorway. I could be a gypsy, traveling through the veins of time. I could be like Lydia, see what she sees, know what she knows, go where she goes to other worlds and other times.

I opened my eyes to find Martin standing in the yard.

Good evening, he said and tipped his hat.

Lydia stirred. She knew his voice. I couldn't speak at first. He pulled off his hat, thinking perhaps I would recognize him, but the light was nearly gone. He stood in silhouette against the sky, lighted only by a cloudy moon, his outline tall and lean.

I asked, Do I know you?

He said, Yes and no.

His voice was so deep and mild and melodic like Lydia's. I could feel her stirring get stronger, dancing, urging me to touch him. She wanted to feel him, and I was her only way.

I had never imagined Lydia an entity all her own. I even told her once I made her up and could erase her if I wanted to. I was picking weeds, pretending she was one of them. I am your thoughts, she laughed, and your weeds. To prove her existence, she whisked me to some other scene, a lush forest I could see and feel and smell and touch and hear. Maybe he came from there, that beautiful place where she had taken me before, where a soul's ghost named Lydia made love to a soul's ghost named Martin. Maybe it all started that way. They were so familiar. Everything about him was memory.

Out here in this little lonesome stretch of meadow and woods, I see lives that few care to imagine. I see maidens rescued. I see pirates gloating over their riches. I see children running across prairies, making love with sunshine. I see me running across prairies making love with the sun, singing with the birds, gloating over the chest of gold I stole from the pirates, being rescued by a gallant prince. Lydia would laugh endlessly at me. But that sundown day she was reaching for the edge of my skin, crawling so close to the air she burned me. She was like lost pearls in a treasure chest daring to be found.

I asked, Where do you come from?

He said, I come from the beginning, just as we all do. We are all travelers, but sometimes we forget where we've been or where we're going.

I always feared Lydia would leave me, or that I would lose her at some point, but I never dreamed how it would happen or that it would come so soon or that I would live beyond it. Martin took my hand and laid me down on the forest floor in a circle of pines. My skin stung like fever. My heart ripped apart. I knew I was losing her but couldn't stop her. I thought I could hold her in, hold on to her forever, but I had no power over the melding of old ghosts.

We laid there in darkness, Martin humming and brushing my hair with his fingers. It was a haunting melody, a minor key. Then he vanished, simply disappeared, and Lydia was gone. I was alone, naked and sweating and sore. Sore in my core, in my chest, between my legs, deep in the places we're forbidden to speak of.

Remembering Lydia is like remembering a story someone told before I could remember stories being told. I pretend when I look out to that line of trees that she and Martin and Leandra and Lanella are all together somewhere while I sit like a shadow on the moon, or maybe in a poem, quietly insane, dressed in a gauzy white smock with lace around my neck and wrists, my hair long and brushed so it curls at the ends, my skin smooth and pale, my body empty of soul.

April 2000

Hey, Richard and Pete,

Just a quick note to say that I really enjoyed your story, Pete. I think Lydia is the perfect example of a soul swirling through multiple lives, and that young girl's was only one of them.

I wonder what my last life was like and where I'll go next because I'm sure I'm not getting it right in this one. I've got more cycling ahead. Was I an insane woman in an institution once, or is that where I'm headed? Was I once a Spanish naval captain, a slave, a queen? How many times have I picked a body and didn't see it through, leaving the parents in agony? Will I be a business owner in the future, an astronaut, a hair stylist, a cab driver? What am I supposed to be right now?

I keep trying to make a plan to move away from here, but my feet are like lead. Sometimes fear stops me. Sometimes pure laziness. Mostly it's indecision. Where to go? What to do? I can't answer these questions, so the open road looks like a trap. No matter where I land, there I am right beside myself doing the same old things and thinking the same old thoughts, evolving at the pace of zero.

Richard, I love your -ation list. Here's one for you straight from the horse's mouth: Stagnation. This is the state in which I live. The Doldrums. Where nothing happens, nothing changes. Even though I'm all over the place physically, I'm frozen mentally. Even though I want to move forward, I'm stuck, halfway lodged in quicksand.

I'm going to have a bottle of wine now and see if there's anything useful at the bottom of it.

Stagnant Sam

June 2000

Dearest Sam and Pete,

I lost Jax at exactly 7:16 this morning. James was moved out by noon. This afternoon someone stole my car. You guys think your lives are mucked. What is this?

I wish we could all move to Pete's paradise and swat the world from our shoulders. I despise Phoenix right now, a place I have always loved. The heat is so ghastly it nearly chokes me. Beverly across the hall is painting. Mix the two smells and get something close to an airborne poison. She has giant sea creatures swimming across the den wall, up over doorways and into other rooms. Everything looks under water. She says it brings her marine-peace in the middle of this dreadful desert. I like it. It makes me want to live there in the dark, cool depths below the cacophony of life.

I never thought I would consider leaving here. Things were comfortable for so long, too long I suppose, and now everything seems upside down. It's not just me. The whole world seems strung out like it's hooked on a drug, hallucinating and flinging people off when gravity slows long enough for another snort.

Therapy was a complete waste. I went once. As for James, the game of Ping-Pong reached an Olympic plateau. It was someone else all along, as I suspected.

Some friend of a friend who kept sneaking in and out of our lives, who says all the right things and makes all the right promises and wears the right shoes and doesn't need so much coddling as I do, as James so eloquently spewed on his way out the door.

In the middle of this chaos, my boss offered me a promotion. I have to respond by Monday morning, so I've got that to think about all weekend. Don't companies usually give promotions without question? I wish this was the case because now I'm forced to consider why I wouldn't want it. My list of cons is exceptionally longer than my list of pros. In work. In life. In love. All at once.

I enjoyed your story, Pete, and I'm especially impressed by your ability to tell it from a young woman's perspective, but I'm still contemplating the idea of a soul's ghost. What is that exactly? I've never heard of this and don't understand how losing Lydia leaves her completely empty of soul if Lydia is only a ghost. What is the difference in a soul and a soul's ghost? Please humor me and explain. And please promise me that dear girl was merely musing, not actually violated by a stranger in the woods. It amazes me how you manage to convey beauty and darkness in the same breath.

There is no beauty shining through the dark in my world at present, only frustration and my perfect new find for the list: agitation. How surprising it wasn't already there.

Our dear Sam, I have a feeling you're going places soon! Things are brightening up for you, I'm sure. Please do let us know where you end up. Maybe we've had it all wrong and it's time we throw this mystery to the wind. What did we decide in our way-back lives? Are we supposed to meet in person? If for no other reason, surely we can cheer each other up.

Fairly agitated,
Richard

August 2000

Sam and Richard,

Note the new address, pen pal people. I'm nowhere near my post office box these days. I've moved yet again but not to paradise. Jamber and I have moved in with my newest love, Alice. I was worn out with the city. She was tired of living alone. We live in a neighborhood. We have a yard.

Alice. Can you believe it? Alice. Not Ally or Al. She writes poems all the time like me. They're tacked up on the fridge and stacked in little piles around the house. I've sent one to a friend who does a modern sort of calligraphy. He's going to write it out on handmade paper and frame it for me, then I'm giving it to her for her birthday next month. Is that romantic overkill or what?

It happened fast, this choice to cohabitate with someone I'd known only weeks. Julz isn't happy about it. Despite her creativity, Alice is a solid executive. I'm a loose artist. How could we possibly have anything in common? Is she using me as a rebound? Is her garage big enough for a studio? Julz questions me to pieces to keep from admitting we've come to our sharpest fork. I'm trying on monogamy, and she can't accept it's not her and that it might fit. I did keep my loft downtown just in case. It may prove beyond me to give my all to only one person.

I have a similar monogamy problem with vision. I can never have only one painting going at a time. I have so many things to say and they come in all these different lights, so I'm at them all at once. In the process there is color and image and structure and space. Illumination. Too bad that can't make the -ation list. Thank God I'm out of my plague phase.

Richard, I'm sorry about James unless it's better for you. And Jax will be back. He's out getting some like me. Meanwhile, add punctuation. And don't ruminate too much on the ghosts of souls. I can't explain. It's just a story, totally make-believe. I don't know or care what it means.

Sam, where on this planet have you ended up?

Creatively yours,
Pete

August 2000

Dear Pete and Richard,

On TV right now they are showing steps of bone. In the core are skulls, long lean bones out then circular, then more skulls, then long bones again. Catacomb. Spirits in the Cathedral of San Francisco. A woman claims there's a presence of someone, moving like wind, a strong presence getting in or out, someone getting somewhere.

There is a sudden physical change, dry leaves whirling and collecting like trash in heaps. Beautiful and translucent gold and brown, then small pieces of snow, like powdered sugar, small specks of cold........... DO WE KNOW EACH OTHER??? Don't you both remember being at a tiny little diner somewhere downtown? Downtown here. Downtown here in Memphis.

We drank coffee, unusually I drank coffee, which should be a sign, and we bolted suddenly for Chicago. At five in the morning, while you guys were sleeping, I stepped outside to ice pitter-pattering down slowly, rain freezing in flight, landing softly with an unrecordable sound. Is this a dream? Or us together in a past life?

God, I swear to God I'm haunted. No matter what I do, no matter where I go, no matter what I think or feel or imagine or bring on or fend off I'm haunted. Or maybe I'm a lost character in one of Pete's stories or a missing comma in a poem.

From the thoroughly haunted Sam Brooks

September 2000

Dearest Sam and Pete,

Tomorrow is my birthday. I might have forgotten if I hadn't received a card from stupid James. Like sending a cheesy card from a drugstore smoothes everything out shiny like a new piece of foil. He enclosed a letter. I refuse to read it. Well, maybe I will later.

I'm feeling quite glum. Jax did come back, thankfully unharmed and oddly perky, but my car didn't survive. It was found wrecked with the tires and other important parts missing, considered totaled, so I've got those details to work out and a new vehicle to buy (and clearly a cat to neuter). Meanwhile, I churn like a hamster on a wheel. I did take the promotion. It's not much more than a title change and a salary bump.

Sam, I am always thrilled to hear from you, but this last time not so much. Your letter was indecipherable, and I'd say you were in the same state when you sent off our copies because surely, surely you wouldn't have sent them had you reviewed your message sober. You know we've never met in person, so you were either drunk or drugged or maybe sleep-writing, complete with a stamp-and-send ending. Whatever it was, I didn't like it. Not one bit.

Our only connection, unless we did make plans in a past life, is *Three Guesses*. Tell us, Pete. What is this painting? I look at it up close and see nothing but colors melting in swirls. From across the room, staring at it until my eyes dry out, I think I see a form. It seems similar to how you described *Wondering Ju*. A woman barely visible walking along water barely visible or something similar. Is it another version? Is it Julz? A soul's ghost? Manhattan on acid? What? I don't want three guesses! I'm not up for rumination, which I added after you told me not to ruminate.

Ruminating,
Richard

October 2000

Richard, I can't explain *Three Guesses*. Paintings, like stories, can't always be explained. I found the photo you sent. It does remind me of *Wondering Ju*, so maybe my *Ju* was the inspiration (already on the list). Julz named it then we sent it out as a donation (not on the list) for exposure back in my earlier days when I was playing with landscapes. A lot of good that did since it sat in storage for years. Then you ended up with it and here we are still because of it. Maybe it came from a dream. Maybe it was a snow dream. Maybe it was a sea dream. Maybe you do have to guess.

Sam, please don't be a druggie. I agree you sounded totally high in your last letter. I didn't like it one bit either.

In the Land of Maybe,
Pete

November 2000

My dear friends Sam and Pete,

I'm tired of dreams. I'm tired of having them. I'm tired of you two talking about them. Dreams are so vague, the ones we picture and the ones of which we have no control. Possibly the ultimate paradox. I have no desire to record my night and nap dreams. I have no desire to remember them. They're odd and broken and flip so fast from one scene to another they make me dizzy. If everyone in them is me then I'm one stripped screw. As if this is news.

At the tail end of Thanksgiving here in the desert, I'm sitting on the deck in my favorite hat enjoying a lovely cabernet sauvignon, spicy and rich like a deep dark cherry soaked in oak with nutmeg and cinnamon, perfect for late fall, though it's barely cool here.

I love wine almost as much as tequila. I love hats and wear them daily. I'm sure this has added to both my joy and my misery. It occurred to me recently that people today don't realize how important and common hats were in previous eras. Look at old photographs. Watch old movies or TV series. Everyone had on a hat when they were out. Men, if they didn't have one on, had one in hand, just removed or ready to put on. Women always had some manner of bling on their heads, even at night before bed and sometimes while they slept.

So, I ask: How is it everyone, even children, wore a hat every day for every activity only decades ago and now we hat wearers look like rebels? I'm not talking winter hats. I'm talking styling hats. I wear this rocking Fedora to the grocery store and people look at me like I'm trying to be something or prove something. Can't I simply enjoy wearing a hat? Bah, humbug! Maybe I'll send you both hats for Christmas. Measure your heads, my friends. Let's make them fit properly!

Styling,
Richard

March 2001

Get out of bed naked.
Dress.
Boil an egg.
Undress.
Shower.
Dress.
Peel egg.
Eat egg.
Clean dishes.
Go visit a friend.
Come home.
Undress.
Walk around naked.
Put on T-shirt and boxers.
Lay on couch.
Sip spiced tea.
Ponder purpose.
Suck peppermint.
Read.
Undress.
Go to bed.
Sleep.
Get out of bed naked and blind.

I woke up blind this morning on purpose. Yesterday the sun blared off the windows across the street. Dust danced in the air above me. But this morning nothing. Experimenting with handicap. Personal research.

Made my way to the bathroom by feeling the walls. Stepped on Jax. Slipped on the rug in the den. Slammed my head on the faucet leaning down to splash water on my face. Half missed the toilet and while trying to find a towel knocked over the toothbrush holder. Barefoot and naked with no idea if my shades were pulled, if anyone was looking in at the blind man groping his way from room to room beating the left side of his head where the radio played. I kept hearing it. Radio noise. The up and down of voices, muffled music, a baseball game, the news. It stayed at the same level no matter where I was, barely audible but there. I heard neighbors talking, dogs snoring. Like they were right here in my kitchen.

Finally, after punching the number in wrong three times… Time 7:42. Temperature 78.

When I counted my steps three times back and forth, I could remember the next time across with more ease. Still, it was alarming. Vertigo is a sense that comes to mind. Dizziness. Balance lost. Tipping over side to side, walking on a beam as wide as the floor, but how could I know how wide? I tried to remember something from tai chi: center of gravity below the belly button, the dan tian, elixir field, source of energy for the body. Mind anchored with breathing to the dan tian. Two inches below the navel.

Time 8:17. Temperature 78.

Democritus the Greek lived among men who no longer believed the gods controlled all. Not long before him, man had come to realize the Nile would rise and recede regardless of the contrivance of gods, that advancing storms were indeed natural occurrences, not angered emotions lashed out from Zeus up high on Mount Olympus. The naturalists were at hand wanting truth, wanting to know what they had seen and experienced was exactly what it appeared to be, not a performance, not a magical illusion.

Democritus the Greek was among them. Democritus the Atomist, profound and unprecedented in his assertions: By convention sweet is sweet, by convention bitter is bitter, by convention hot is hot, by convention cold is cold, by convention color is color. But in truth there are atoms and the void.

He believed atoms were small rapid things, different in shape, which in turn decided their action, that something sour and prickly on the tongue must have atoms with sharp points moving jaggedly, that something like cool water must have rounded atoms slipping in and around with ease. Atoms and void. Atoms and void. Atoms and void.

Democritus the Atomist. I am convinced he was blind for at least a day because indeed there are atoms and void. The atoms of the coffee table corners are most definitely barbed.

Time 11:33. Temperature 78.

One two three four five six seven eight nine ten eleven twelve thirteen fourteen fifteen stairs. As anal as I am about counting things, I had never counted the stairs. Sometimes I sit and count out a minute to feel it completely. We say time is slow, time is fast, too much time, too little time, no time at all, all the time in the world. So, for therapy and sometimes lucidity, I count sixty seconds. The glorified minute. I set out to count all of the seconds in one hour but grew too anxious trying to cram words like *onethousandtwohundredseventyseven* into one single second of time.

It's tiring what all the mind sees when the eyes don't, the third eye ecstatic I suppose for so much undivided attention. All other senses are enhanced when vision is void. I was forced to confront philosophies without words, quiet revelations, demons, regrets, wishes, structure and space, color and no color, fears. By midday, strange recipes of paranoia measured out when I walked from room to room, fear I was losing my mind, fear I would truly become blind, fear I would stumble over nothing on the floor and fall and split my head open and be found dead and naked in the foyer with a black mask over my eyes.

Evening came with my upstairs neighbor, who generally slams his door around nine. I quit calling time and temp, didn't care anymore what hour was ticking or what it was like outside. Rain was coming, an oddity all its own. I could smell it.

I sang "Amazing Grace" and Jax went crazy circle-eighting me and nipping at my ankles. He also does this when I whistle. Resonance. Perhaps whistle atoms are round, moving in and around his soul with ease, which would say the atoms of the soul are round also, don't you think? Democritus would applaud. I understand why singers close their eyes. I could see the emotion. I could see the story. I cried at the end…was blind but now I see.

I've waited until midnight to pull off the mask. My equilibrium is shot. At least I can see now with the faint light coming in from the street lamps, from the glow coming off the computer screen. For reasons I cannot define, I feel inclined to share this though it probably makes absolutely no sense. I'm sending it anyway, about to hit Print and go put your envelopes in the box.

Where are you people? Oddly enough, this curious connection is the only thing I look forward to anymore. Please don't you have wonderful musings to share?

Weary from experimentation (too many bloody syllables),
Richard

April 2001

Hi, guys! As you can see, the sky is tie-dyed here in
Iowa. Sorry for quick postcards. Just wanted you to
know I haven't fallen off the face of the earth. Dad is
forwarding my mail. I promise to write more soon!

Hugs,
Sam

May 2001

The moon hangs fat and white, bulging from the sky like an eye passing over to give the world a stare. Jamber sits at the window looking like a talisman from somewhere wild and wicked. Only the sound of his purring fills the empty space. Tense purring, not calm. Me being awake in the hours I'm supposed to be sleeping disturbs him because he can't sneak around and paw at my hair like he does when I'm dreaming.

Alice is traveling for work, so it's just us out here unnerved by a great horned owl staring in. Why is it here? Is it real or imagined? It doesn't screech, doesn't move, sits firmly planted deep in the old tree that looms over us, a huge creature, its head turned sideways as if studying how to get through the window to snatch up Jamber for a late-night snack.

A grocery list rings loud in my head in rhymes (red peppers for roasting, rye bread for toasting) along with regret about a lie I told Alice (a small but terrible lie) and doubts about a letter I sent to Julz (a short but terrible letter) and images of people I don't know, made up characters in a disjointed play.

I see an old man at the laundromat laying his wet towels straight and even in the dryer, one on top of the other. Nearby, three gypsy women giggle and point at him, low whispering in a mystical language. Rich smells from the Chinese restaurant next door drift in and mix with the heat. Church bells chime thirteen times, and no one notices. The towels stick together in their rotation. The old man stares blankly at them through the scarred window, his method failing. The women continue to giggle and point.

Down the street, Barbra stands over a bowl and stirs without looking. Chicken salad minus celery. She hates celery and substitutes pickles instead. She stops to consider adding another pickle, decides yes, then loses it to the floor. She sees this as a sign. She sees everything as a sign. The tattered grocery bag fluttering in the tree: Demise. The picture in the hall of a long-gone lover: Denial. The pickle laying splat on the floor: Decline.

She stares out the window. Tommy walks by and gives her house a quick glance. Tommy walks by every day with his right hand fisted and shaking, mumbling furiously: Delirium. She slinks away to her den filled with dying plants and old *Life* magazines, leaving the salad unfinished on the counter: Decay.

Above her, Lin lays on the porch studying the undersides of leaves, popcorn on the floor, cat toys behind the bookshelf, streaks of sun coming through chair legs, gnats swarming, a penny, a rubber band. There on the floor, hidden behind the screen, she regards the clouds passing, all the world's faces caught moving across the sky. She sees Tommy walk past shaking his fist. She hears Barbra's radio downstairs airing the news. She watches their neighbor Fran traipse down the sidewalk avoiding the cracks. She sees Chester, who claims Fran is crazy not well in the head, watering his yard. This is exactly how he says it: That Fran is crazy not well in the head.

Scowling, Chester watches Fran. He looks up and spots Lin. Lin the crip, he calls her. Lin the crip who walks with a limp, who lays up there on the porch floor peeking down through the screen at him tending his yard. CHESTER'S YARD. He has this sign posted at the edge of his porch. So that no one will confuse where his yard ends and Fran's yard begins, he has put another sign on the invisible line between them that runs thin and straight. FRAN'S YARD. Last spring, Chester cut down the two old oak trees between them. Now his crooked porch roof shows, and his dirty white house with faded black shutters looks lopsided.

Fran ignores her neighbors spying and click-click-clicks to the grocery in heels from another decade. She walks with a long stride, which isn't natural for her build. It doesn't look natural in her steps, but the effort makes her feel more visible, more knowing. Swinging on her shoulder is a bright red bag she bought for shopping. People stare at a person dropping things into a bright red bag. They wish they had one, a bag like that, loosely woven so food shows through somewhat rude and elegant all at once. They wish they had long strides and confidence, a sign announcing their yard, neighbors watching them click-click-click to the store.

Hayes stares out the big window at old houses lined up like dominoes. He imagines the conversations going on inside. In the middle is Chester's house, uglier now without the trees. A white cat passes through hazy streetlamp shadows. A pathetic candy cane still hangs along the corridor, burning faded lights. A lonely snowman hangs nearby burning none, thinking there must still be a land called Once Upon A Time where he belongs instead of hanging dull and filthy on a light pole. Hayes closes his shade to banish the forgotten ornaments from his view. He pushes the window out an inch to hear the swishing of cars on moist pavement.

I want these strangers out of my head. I want to sleep. Jamber wants me to sleep.

> Curious cat names: Mouse, Monkey, Mole, Mud
> Odd dog names: Bill, Barber, Buss, Bane
> Fish: Hoss, Hoover, Herb, Ham

> Song for the story about Hal and Harriet:
>
> I lost her in a storm on the eve of St. Patty's
> Gone away to the land of rest.
> I will see her on the lea on the eve of St. Patty's
> Wearing lace on the hem of her dress.

> Someday I will join her on the eve of St. Patty's

Fly away to the land of rest.
I will kiss her ever gentle on the eve of St. Patty's
Lay my head on the swell of her breast.

Lin lays in the hammock tapping her feet against the frame to jazz filtering up from downstairs. Tommy saunters past shaking his fisted hand, giggles at the lick of a sax solo outburst and moves on mumbling. Hayes peeks through his bathroom window into Barbra's bedroom.

It's early May and cool with the moon chasing Venus. Chester speed-rocks on his front porch watching Fran eating pasta and drinking wine on her front porch with the man who comes for dinner on Saturdays. The one-eyed man, Chester calls him. The one-eyed man who walks loose and bow-legged like a cowboy. Lin thinks the one-eyed man is aloof and mysterious with his black patch and dark skin. They are laughing, he and Fran, louder than they should be, but it's show. Everything with Fran is show.

During the two minutes I slipped into sleep, the owl crept closer to the window, uncomfortably closer even though thick, leaded glass separates us. Jamber mews his discontent and leaps from the windowsill to the bed to the window again. I lay here still awake, which irritates him more than the owl. I can't imagine what else he must do through the night so secretive.

The first bit of dawn arrives. Another brief moment

of sleep is scarred by the sound of the street sweeper beeping and swishing its brooms. The owl is gone. The morning is damp and chilly. Jamber, pressed against my back, moves an inch to cover his ears with his tail.

A lawn mower cranks up. I can't tell if it's coming from outside my window or inside my head, from my real neighbor's yard or from Chester's yard, preened and leaning toward the sidewalk where Fran walks by clicking so hard her steps echo fiercely off crooked porch roofs and metal screens. Tommy passes by mumbling with his head down. Dogs bark. Garbage trucks screech. Lin peeks out from behind her plants. Hayes spies on Barbra, who hears the crooning of a siren: Disaster.

The old man's towels are finally dry. One by one he pulls them from the heat, folds them straight and even, stacking one on top of the other. Lined up along the dryers, the gypsies watch and hum a strange melody in a minor key.

The moon is gone. The sun is here. I need coffee. Percolation.

Percolating,
Pete

July 2001

Hello, dear friends.

I've been staring at *Three Guesses* all morning. Can you believe we've been at this for three years now? How surreal is that? I wish we would at least agree on email. Or, for heaven's sake, get on a phone call. Imagine what it would be like to *talk* to each other! I can easily set up conference calls through work.

We must engage in these real-time options soon because I'm bored and anxious. It's important I hear something logical from you two soon, not another cryptic insomnia bit (which I did rather enjoy) or a brief tie-dyed message (which I did not enjoy at all). Remind me you're out there, that you're real people and not storied characters in my head like the ones Pete carries around in his. Otherwise, it's clear I've gone off my goose.

Quickly please,
Richard

September 2001

Hello? Sam? Pete? Is anybody out there?!?

My turn for postcards, though it pains me to think we've reduced our relationship to a 4 x 6 platform instead of moving forward with the technology right at our fingertips. This is getting ridiculous, especially with you, Sam. Are you okay? Seriously, write today please! I'm downright perturbed.

Perturbation. Look it up, people. Result of anxiety.

Yours,
Richard

October 2001

Sir Richard of Arizona, are you British? Sometimes you come off like some haughty Londoneer. But how can that be if you grew up in California? Doesn't add up, my friend. Doesn't add up.

I realize it's been like a year or more since I last shared any real news with you two. I don't know where time goes. I can't account for any of it. Life with Alice feels like a slow read. Days pass. Weeks pass. Months pass. We like each other then we don't then we do again. It's a never-ending spin cycle. She wants more than I can give, so I try harder, which is ridiculous because she isn't trying at all anymore.

I'm not sure how much longer this will last, but for now I need to stay put. NYC is in turmoil. Julz is thankfully unharmed and other people I know were not directly affected, but we're all affected in some way. All of us will forever remember exactly where we were on the morning of 9-11-2001. It's devastating beyond belief. I've heard so many stories, but until I'm back in the city and see things for myself, I'll keep them to myself so I'm not spreading hearsay. It's hard to know what is and isn't true from out here.

One thing I do know to be true is that your absence, Sam Brooks, is now beyond ridiculous. I didn't want to be a part of this from the beginning, yet here I am better at it than you. Where are you? Iowa, really? I don't think so. Where are you hiding? What piece of fringe are you hanging from?

Fimbriation. Look it up, people. Rule of tincture.

Yours sometimes,
Pete

February 2002

Richard, did I lose you by being such a jerk? Sam, have we lost you altogether? The holidays have passed. Even Groundhog Day has passed. Write please, both of you immediately, or I'm done with this.

Pete

February 2002

Sam, seriously, what's up? Where are you? Is this over? I've been impatiently awaiting word from you before writing again, but time's up. My next letter will be addressed to The Father of Sherry 'Sam' Brooks asking what's happened to you!

Pete, no I am not some haughty British bloke, though it could be in my ancestry. Mabry is definitely English. If I wanted to waste valuable time, I could scour through all of our letters and evaluate the way you sound at times, so bug off on the criticism. I'm grateful to hear you were out of the city on 9-11, but I'm irritated with the barb, not to mention your blatant misspelling. It's Londoner, for heaven's sake, not Londoneer. If you're going to be haughty yourself, at least check your grammar.

In case you can't tell, I'm extremely upset about the decline in our correspondence, and I'm doubly upset we haven't heard back from you, Sam. At this point, I'm downright worried.

Completely unsettled,
Richard

May 2002

Dear Pete and Richard, my best unmet friends on the planet,

I am so sorry for bailing for so long! Truly I am! I did sort of fall off the face of the earth, or maybe I fell right onto it face first. I'm not sure what you might call all of this. I've been getting your letters from Dad, who has about lost his mind keeping up with me. Apologies over and over for causing you worry. I wanted to reach out, but time kept passing, and I kept not being ready to share until now.

I was pretty much forced out of my stupor and hit the road like a vagabond. I won't get into all of my travels, just some key scenes of interest. This will take some time. Are you sitting down? Here goes…

In early October 2000, on a Wednesday afternoon right in the middle of a wicked thunderstorm, something crazy came over me and I fell into bed with a total stranger—a beautiful Australian man, if you can believe that, in town on business with a company I was temping for as a receptionist. Something went off in me the second he walked in the door and up to my desk, like nothing I'd ever felt before. I mean, we both knew something was going to happen. It was almost visibly hanging in the air between us.

When he left after the meeting, I got up and walked right out the door behind him and got into his car. We drove two miles an hour in a deluge to his hotel without saying a single word. Still silent, I followed him like a puppy into his room and immediately abandoned every fear I'd ever had about sex with a stranger. I had never felt so beautiful in all my life, or more careless. I never told anyone. I can't believe I'm telling you, but you have to know about that part to hear the biggest part of this crazy story. Seriously, sit down if you aren't already.

I have a baby! Well, she's not so much a baby now and her name is Leeci, like Lee-see, and she is truly the most incredible thing I've ever experienced in my life. So beautiful. So precious. She made her worldly entrance last July outside a place called Lupe's Diner in Somewhere, Iowa.

I know your jaws are dropped wide open. You probably think I'm nuts. Believe me, I thought the same thing. I was already on the edge, as you probably guessed, then I lost my job with the agency. You can't walk out on an assignment like that, especially with a client, and expect to get it back or any others in the future. I picked up another job with a caterer then realized one night during a particularly chaotic event that my period hadn't come, and I'm as regular as they come in that regard. Three pregnancy tests later, motherhood was undeniably confirmed.

I can't begin to describe my state of mind at that

point. I had no idea what to do, but aborting or giving up a baby seemed ludicrous no matter how many ways I played it out, but it seemed just as ludicrous to keep it. (I didn't know 'it' was a girl until she arrived).

The same questions slammed me over and over. What if I fail at being a mom? I certainly didn't have a decent role model. How will I do this alone? I've never even been around children and have no close family or friends with kids to give me advice or come running when I fall apart with fear or depression or confusion or worse, anger. How will I make a living? Do people even hire pregnant women? My savings account will carry me only so long then what? How will I pay for a child? How much does it cost to have one? How do I get family insurance? Is there even a way to do that without a job? Will Dad help me? What if he shuns me?

I could go on and on with the torment, but I'm sure you get the picture. It was pure agony trying to sort it all out in my tired brain and decide what to do. And time was running out, literally, for me to make a decision. Then it started to rain. Really hard. I was curled up on the couch hiding from the world under a blanket. Dad called and left a message about going to visit Colton's sister in Kentucky for Thanksgiving and asked me to go with them. It was a last-minute trip. They were leaving the next morning. And that's when it all sank deep with me, the unpredictability of life. It drenched me like the rain was falling inside my apartment on top of me. Right then and there I knew I was going to have this baby, period, and not tell anyone, not for a while anyway.

In March, I was working a second part-time job in a small grocery store and my little secret was getting harder to hide. I felt desperate to get out of town. I was nowhere near ready to share this with Dad, who I managed to avoid in all that time, even at Christmas. He went to Kentucky again with Colton. He didn't need me.

I faked a family emergency (uncomfortably close to the truth) and quit both jobs and hit the road. The morning I left, the sky behind me was sunny. Ahead of me was dark, thunderstorm gray. Suntears is what my mom used to call the mix of half stormy half sunny days. She would stop everything to watch a day like that pass. Wild skies, wild clouds splitting and chasing the sun, she would say. Probably she would also say going on a road trip pregnant was running away and that I've been running my whole life from someone or something that doesn't suit me. But who is she to have an opinion? Did I ever tell you she killed herself? Seriously, did we plan for that experience in some other life?

Anyway, I wouldn't exactly call it running. I wasn't running from anything in particular. And in my warped state of mind, being pregnant and on the road alone didn't occur to me as terribly dangerous or unstable.

Besides, every midsize town in the Midwest had a mid-wife willing to give me a checkup. They thought being pregnant on the road alone was an erratic maneuver. "Where is the father?" was the first question. The second was, "Who is the father?" And third, when I refused to answer the first two, "Do you know who the father is?" Yes, I know who he is. His name is Jan Gaynes. He's Australian, and I'll never see him again. To date, you two are the only ones who know his name.

I managed to find work here and there. People were skeptical, but sympathy won over the more pregnant I got. I spent Easter at the Waffle House with a couple of truckers. One of them stopped me in the parking lot to point out that my front passenger tire was low. Another one pointed out that all four needed to be replaced. They insisted on buying me lunch then aired up my tires and filled my gas tank. A charming start to motherhood, right?

I was over seven months when I landed at Lupe's Diner in the middle of Iowa. I stopped for lunch and met the owners Marena and Ezzy. They were shocked I was out and about pregnant and downright homeless. I didn't mention to them or anyone else I could jump back across the Mississippi River any time and go to Dad's.

They offered their garage apartment if I could help with some basic chores, so I agreed and moved in with my two bags of belongings. They doted on me like mothers, more than my own mother ever did. They took me to a clinic for an ultrasound. I made everyone promise to keep the gender a secret from me. My baby was fine and exactly the right size. I felt great physically. Then, eight months in, my feet swelled up. I could barely walk. I couldn't breathe, couldn't stop sweating. I couldn't sit up or lay down or find any comfortable position whatsoever. I'm telling you this because as men you don't and won't ever have any idea what pregnancy is like.

The most comfortable thing around was an old rocker on the front porch of the diner, and that's where I was planted the afternoon Leeci made her debut. We were talking about tobacco because Ezzy was smoking a big fat cigar and Marena was getting on to her about it. Ezzy said, "To grow a good tobacco plant, you've got to pluck stuff off it like flowers and suckers and worms. You've got to hang it straight to cure, put a fire under it, chop it, grind it, mold it. It takes a long time to make a good cigar." She said it's a lot like raising kids, minus the chop and grind part, and patted my belly. At the same time, Leeci gave a big stir and nearly knocked me out of the chair. An hour later there she was, all pink and blue and screaming like crazy. She was perfect.

Marena and Ezzy would have kept us forever, especially with the state of things after 9-11 (so relieved you and Julz are okay, Pete!). We did stay through New Year's, but I had no desire to raise Leeci in some Iowa corn field, even though it was really beautiful there. I was restless and ready to move on. They put new tires on my car and sent us off with huge grandma tears. I planned to go straight to Dad's, but then we found Claire, or she found us. It depends on who is telling the story. We weren't far from home, less than two hours, when I saw an old house turned into an antique shop. I pulled up right when a woman was locking the door. I begged her to open back up and sell me the quilt hanging in the front window. It was all the shades of blue sewn in waves. It felt like a sign.

I can't explain the conversation Claire and I ended up in or why I spilled out my life story to her, but we agreed Leeci and I should stay with her for a week or two. I wasn't ready to face Dad, and Leeci needed some wide-open spaces. Her house was perfect, bright and clean with carpeted floors. Leeci was in heaven rolling and crawling around.

Claire was like a grandmother hen for me, a great-grandmother for Leeci. She made me get up with her early in the mornings and watch the sun come up from the back porch, no matter how cold it was. She said sunrise is the perfect time for reflection, and she thought I had lots of that to do. She reserved stargazing for more serious contemplation (new one, Richard?) and said, "Pick a place and stare until you see what's really there." The first time I did this I knew I couldn't settle down at home. We would visit Dad, then no more wandering. I had to pick a destination, get there and stay put.

Leeci and this roadtripping has changed me. By now you know how I think and what I think, so it's not hard to imagine I see things differently. The morning we left Claire's, the sky turned wild with Suntears. I pulled over to sit and watch the purple-gray clouds circling the sun. Leeci was asleep and breathing so hard her lips popped open with every exhale. I watched her little frame rising and falling in rhythm with the coming storm. What a gift. What a precious, incredible gift.

I wonder if my mom ever thought that about me. I wonder what made her leave me, why she deserted me. I wonder why we planned a reunion that wasn't going to last. I considered how it would feel to leave Leeci, but she opened her eyes right then and gave me a dreamy look, reminding me I would never ever abandon my daughter like my mom abandoned hers.

I can't explain having a child, the physical labor or the aftereffects of sudden motherhood. It's true what they say. You don't just love your child. You're IN love with your child. Claire said to be easy and calm and thoughtful and Leeci would be the same. She's convinced life isn't nearly as hard as we make it, herself included. She said children are magic.

It's true. Leeci is magic. Dad thinks she's magic. We did finally make it to him after a few more weeks with Claire. She practically kicked us out. She said it was time. Leeci was growing fast, and Dad was so close, and he had spent another Christmas without me.

He was too depressed to be a real parent after my mom checked out. He never spent time with me. He let me be too free. But with Leeci he is so careful, so lit up. She is a breath of air and energy for him. He's begged us to stay, at least through her first birthday, but too many signs to mention point to the sea and its wind, its strong cleansing wind.

We set out across Tennessee early Wednesday morning then across North Carolina. By sunset on Friday, we'll be lying on the sands of the Outer Banks thinking of nothing but what the sea breezes have to say. Claire used to go there every summer to visit family and connected me with her cousin Anna, so we do have a place to stay, at least for a little while. I'm a bit terrified. I have no particular plan, but I have a strong feeling it will unfold just as it should.

You can close your mouths now! Please let me hear back from both of you soon. I'll get my actual address to you when I have one. For now, still send your letters to Dad's. I can hear him now calling me to come down for lunch.

By the way, it's Mother's Day today. Wow! Who imagined I'd ever be one?!?

For sure, Richard, add impregnation.

Much love,
Sam

May 2002

Dearest Sam and Pete,

This is where I draw the line on this archaic form of communication. Why did we ever decide that? I know, I know I was solid about it early on, but forget all this business about keeping to letters only. It's imperative we all agree to move on from this time-draining system. We should have long before now. Even if we never agree to meet in person, we should immediately agree to emails and phone calls. If we had done this sooner, you could have called either of us at any time, Sam. You could have come to Phoenix. I would have given you the entire upstairs.

I am in complete awe that you have a child. Leeci Brooks. How beautiful! Does she have a middle name? Thank goodness you're okay, both of you, and back with us. Meanwhile, here's a camera. Start clicking. And make triples of everything so we all have copies.

Amazing, isn't it, how quickly things can happen? Lightning through a tree. Slick pavement. Keys dropped in a grate. Eyes locked across a room. A child. Go forth, my dear. Continue to be brave and you will find your peaceful sanctuary in this psycho world.

I'll share my current decision in trying to find peace. I'm going primitive, low maintenance, tossing things out. I've been through every cabinet, drawer, and closet.

Who needs all this stuff? I've found things I can't imagine keeping, things tucked away like memories waiting to be rediscovered and mulled over. It feels good to purge. Even though I don't know if I would, I, too, could pick up and go with little notice.

Pete gets my great-aunt's vinegar jar. Sam gets wind chimes and Leeci a tambourine.

Sending love on the wind in all directions!
Richard

June 2002

Sam, I am still picking my jaw off the floor. Please forever call her Leeci. Not chopped to Lee or Ci, not LB or LC. Leeci is perfect and lovely. I know she must be soft and indescribable. The world is graced with yet another beautiful woman.

You'll always have someone now. Unless there's Pete Wren offspring out there oblivious to me, I will die old and alone without any kids and in the end without a woman at my side I suppose. If I could have a child already grown up and comfortably in friendship with me, I would have a son. I could never have a daughter. I would keep such a thumb on her, overprotect her from jerks like me. But I'm far from giving into a lifetime of compromise.

I doubt I will ever truly love the deepest kind of love. Julz is the closest I've come. I tried with Alice. She was so tolerant and open, for a while at least, but also aloof. Something about me didn't click completely for her and likewise for me. I think initially for me it was something stupid like the part in her hair or what she wore to bed or how long she took to shower. Some idiotic peeve I can't place but couldn't tolerate. Then we started the infinite spin cycle, so use the PO box again. I'm back in the city. I have missed this cranky old place, and I think it's missed me.

I'm in a new loft, much bigger than before, which I can afford now because something incredible happened. Three months ago, I received the Grayson Abbott Fellowship Award for "demonstrating experimental initiative, progressive vision, and an intimate perspective in the arts." Can you believe this? Pete Wren is now a household name! In the art world at least. All on a fluke. All from *Without Warning*. I started and stopped the series over and over then finally hit it headlong and finished with eight more, the same woman falling.

I've gotten all this lip from women's organizations, hardcore feminists claiming I'm taking advantage of tragedy. One group challenged me publicly to give my prize money and any future profits from the series to abused women shelters. I declined. In one interview, I asked the interviewer when she pursued this angle what tragedy didn't make somebody a little better off in the end. This didn't go over well. But life is art. Art is life. A woman was pushed from a window. I captured it in paint nine times. Big deal. Big reward!

If these twits would get their heads out of a hole, maybe they could hear me about the symbolism of falling, how it can mean losing control of something or within something. The series is not tee-totally about violent death, which I've explained ad nauseam. Guess what people! Our falling lady might get a grip on her situation before hitting the ground! And guess what else! We're in NYC, a.k.a. New York Crazy. Weird crazy things like this happen every day! At least the GA Fellowship gets it. The haters need to get over it.

Three universities have called asking me to appear in seminars and class lectures. Isn't it funny how people use words? One uppity dean called and said, "We would love for you to appear in the Cecil Conner Lecture Series." Me or my art? Which gets to appear? If it's me personally, do I get to pop onto stage from behind a velvet curtain? Abracadabra! The artist appears! I honestly don't care how I get on stage. I told her what my appearance would cost and she agreed without argument, so I increased my fee with the next request. I've never made this kind of money in my life!

Julz is sulking over the whole thing. Another gallery gets credit for the series even though she showed the first one, and ingeniously at that. She hung it in the middle of a huge window on the west wall. My falling woman melted into the building in the background and people talked about it for weeks. Articles were written. Then we had another major falling out, so I moved it to the Copper Bull Gallery down the street then finished the series. All of this was going on while I was with Alice, so it's like a double-edged sword at both our necks.

I mention Julz in every interview. I even hear myself say, "I wouldn't be here today if not for Julie Reese." I say it every time, but she never hears it or at least claims she hasn't. I'm not sure where we are. She's the only woman I could imagine sitting old on a bench with. Maybe we'll figure it out one day.

I'm sorry not to elaborate on the joy of Leeci, but I don't know children or how to talk about them or what to even ask about them. I don't remember much of my childhood. Chosen blockage. As you know, it was not a good one. And I'm truly sorry yours ended up motherless. What a despicable thing to do. She didn't deserve someone as good as you. I wouldn't worry one bit if she would consider your travels "running away."

I've done a lot of running myself. The first time it was the best thing I ever did. Other times not so much. And just when I thought I might run again, all of this success happened with the WW series. Running has consequences, some good and some bad. Not running has them too. You will find your cleansing wind. Perhaps Leeci is the teasing breeze. Give her a long gaze from me. And yes, you must send pictures!

Richard, the old vinegar jar is perfect, like a piece of art itself, and Sam's wind chimes inspired the enclosed vignette.

I hope all continues to go well for us all, that we find peace and happiness in this crazy world without warnings.

Add ostentation.

Yours in ostentatious fame,
Pete

"Passage to Memory"
by Pete Wren

The sun falls and with it a warm breeze hinting spring. Now only blue-gray shadows. A fan blowing lazy and slow. Colored glass pieces tinkling from strings tied to a twig.

Mona lays on her side and rubs her palm across her thigh. "He'll be coming soon," she tells the clouds and sips another sip. Already the candles are burning low. There can be no other light. They can't remember each other too clearly.

Belle clings to the windowsill, staring at other cats lounging in the yard. Mona doesn't know she's found a way out, so Belle must act sad and thoughtful in the way cats do when they are keeping something hidden.

"My precious pretty thing," Mona croons, almost whispering, and moves from the couch to fill her glass again. "He'll be coming soon, and then what will you watch?"

Headlights pour through the screen and dance on bare walls. Tonight the moon is hiding in the corner of a sky thick as black velvet. A train moving across the river wails its passage, marking the time.

Belle loves the candles glowing in the dark. She can see ghosts in this room, vapors hanging in the air collecting like dust on the shelves. Most of them resemble Mona in stretches of her life, gauzed memories. A ghost cat white as flour is curled up on the radiator, wrapped by a long skinny tail.

Mona can't see the ghosts or hear them, but Belle imagines she can feel them. Mona gets caught in their whispering but thinks it's only the wind.

"He'll be coming soon," mocks the one who looks like an old Mona. "And then what will you watch?" She giggles shrill and pokes the ghost cat in the side. "Move away from there, old fool. You're taking all the heat."

He shudders at her touch and curls up tighter.

Belle watches in fascination as the ghost floats about the room poking the others. They shudder as though a whiff of cold air has rushed through the door, but there is only a soft breeze, only an old spook poking and prodding.

"Should I tell you about my friend Ruby who died on the train?"

"No," they hiss together.

She flies in and out of the doors opened out to the porch.

"What about the couple who lived next door to me for so long, the Wyndells, who died in the fire?"

"No!" a little louder.

"Sylvia Gamble who drowned in front of her children?"

"NO!" they screech, and Belle can't imagine Mona not hearing them.

"Oh, shoo, all of you!" the old ghost whimpers and lands on the couch.

Mona slides back into the candlelight, swaying and spilling champagne on the rug. She reaches out to the door, to the street, beckoning. The old ghost forgets her stories and moves with the grace of warm air to swirl around Mona, caressing her stringy curls, blowing the hairs on her arms.

"He'll be coming soon," she sings in Mona's ear.

"He'll be coming soon," Mona sings back, holding out her arms, swaying to the tinkling of colored glass pieces hanging from strings tied to a twig.

August 2002

standing in wind
standing complete in it
standing in awe

it goes around
and through
straight through

the sky is as immense as anything has ever been
hidden only by horizons
kissing them while everything breaks away

anything that was everything before
slips into nothing but the wind
and the sound of wind
the awe of wind
and its wisdom
the breath of wind
and its cleansing

Have you ever stood on a raw stretch of beach with
the wind blowing sand so hard it stings your legs? I
can see now how islands move, how dunes are created,
how they shift, how people come to places like this and

never leave. It nearly blows me down, the wind. And it is so cleansing! It seems to move right through me, cleaning me out but filling me up at the same time.

Why have I not been on the Outer Banks my whole life? Why didn't my soul pick here from the start? The poem, if that's what it is, is as close to describing this place as I can get. I feel happily drenched with Atlantic winds. And you can see forever. The clouds are like storybook shapeshifters, or huge colonies of ghosts making their way to heaven, if there is such a thing. The ocean is hypnotizing and comes to the shore at an angle, sneaking up on it like love sneaks up on us, coming in from the side where we can't see it head-on.

We live on the sound side in Hatteras on the bottom floor of Anna's house and spend lots of time on the beach where we can see boats way out to sea, maybe as far as the channel on clear days, though probably the earth is too curved from here to there. Leeci learned to walk on the sand the day we arrived. She took up chasing after a piper like she'd always walked. I wish I had it on video. I wish I had hours and hours of video for her to watch when she's older. She is so full up with happiness day after day. People stop and stare at her babbling with the birds. Tourists compliment her red-blond curls and can't get over her eyes, green as the sea. She talks to the miniature crabs and whatever other creatures are skedaddling across the sand. She wants to live in the water, but the waves are tremendous and the riptides are terrifying, so I don't let her go in past her ankles, and I'm always right there with her.

She doesn't look a thing like me. I think she looks like Jan Gaynes, but I can feel him easier than I can see his face. I haven't been with anyone since. And I'm wishing like crazy he would pull up to shore on a little boat from all the way down under. Would I love or despise him? Would I even like him? There was no time to get to know him. I wonder how he would feel knowing this beautiful child came from him. Maybe Leeci has a dozen half-siblings around the world, but it didn't feel like our encounter was commonplace. It all happened so crazy, like it was destined to bring her to me.

I love your story, Pete, and I love the chimes, Richard. You know Leeci adores the tambourine. Sometimes I have to hide it because the gulls love it too. When she takes it out, they clamor around like she's feeding them something. Feeding them music. The crows hate it. All except the one who's adopted us. You have to imagine the immense size and blackness of the crows here. Crumb (see, we even named the fool thing) is the blackest black with corn-gold eyes. And he's huge. Hawk-sized. Leeci feeds him breadcrumbs, which he merely picks at to suit her. Anna says to try peanuts. Crumb pretends to protect us. He knows when we're headed to the beach, follows along above us. When we get there, he caws at gulls who swoop too close and badgers people who come up to talk to us. It's kind of hysterical.

Sometimes he makes me crazy, but Crumb is part of the family now. I sent Dad some pictures of the three of us, and he sent one to my high school when they mailed a form requesting current info. I was a loner all through school. I'm sure they hardly remember Sherry Brooks and are unimpressed by my odd choice of pets. The drama teacher Mr. Kimball might remember me. He would think Crumb is keen.

It's one in the morning here on the Outer Banks and I'm bushed. I work nights at a restaurant on the harbor. This is unprecedented, right? Me a waitress! Packing a tray of plates is tricky, but I'm getting good at it. Balance comes with the territory after a few spills. Leeci stays with Anna while I work. This was a stipulation of my lease. (Is that one on the list?) We love her. She loves us. Another mother for me, another grandmother for Leeci. Seems we've had so many and none of them blood kin. I am so blessed. Marena and Ezzy, Claire, and now Anna, you guys and Leeci, my greatest treasure.

Okay, that's all for now. I need to get off Anna's computer and back downstairs to my sleeping sweetheart. Write soon!

Love you like water loves sun,
Sam

October 2002

Thank you for the pictures, Sam! Leeci is so beautiful it almost hurts to look at her too long. Pete, you must paint her in some way.

Please tell us how you fared with Gustav! I've been so worried and wish I could have called you, but we need to collectively agree on stretching this beyond old-fashioned snail mail.

Jax and I head to Doras in a week to stay with Mother for a while and make a plan, so use the new return address until further notice. I quit my job and sold my condo and almost everything in it except *Three Guesses*, which you should receive by Friday, Sam. I hope you don't mind me springing it on you, and fingers crossed you have a place for it. To note, stipulation is already on the list.

I'll share more once I get settled.

Love to all,
Richard

November 2002

Sam, I can't believe I'm doing this since Christmas presents are absolutely not my thing, but enclosed is an early one for Leeci. I don't care if she opens it now or waits until Christmas Day. Nothing for you, Richard, sorry.

I've never painted a crow before and never will again. It was painful to create something so lifelike. It will not win me any awards except hopefully that of Leeci's heart.

This is my time of year to disappear. I'll be back on the other side of these wretched holidays.

Pete

December 2002

Hey, guys! Isn't it funny how life turns? *Three Guesses* now hangs in my little den, and how wonderful it is even if we are still guessing what it is. Thank you so much, Richard. I can't imagine what it cost you to ship it here! I'm so sorry I didn't write immediately when it was delivered, but hopefully you got confirmation it arrived. And Leeci does absolutely love the crow painting, Pete. It looks just like Crumb.

What incredible gifts! Thank you both beyond words!!!

I've been working crazy hours. Maybe tourists disappear this time of year, but the locals keep us busy. I'm lucky Marco's is a year-round hangout. A lot of businesses shut down until March and even part of April.

Winter is eerie here, and it's only the beginning. The surf has turned crusty and bluish-gray in places. The parking lots are deserted. The wind is hard and piercing cold. Anna warned me about the rough stuff, but she forgot to tell me about the snow geese that come. She forgot to tell me about harvesting oysters in the sound.

Before the cold set in, we traveled up and down Highway 12 to get our bearings. See the map on the enclosed brochure and find Hatteras at the very bottom. We visited all the small towns above it (Frisco, Buxton, Avon, Waves, Rodanthe) and then headed north to Nags Head and Jockey's Ridge where people hang glide. I'm definitely doing that next summer! Further up is Duck and Corolla, and from there the world seems to end.

Southwest of Hatteras is Ocracoke Island. I would live there except the only way on and off is by ferry, and I'm not up for that with a little one. It's a magical island, an old fishing village with all kinds of haunts and lots of artists. I got creative myself and made three shell wind chimes that I put in a little shop called Shorebags. One actually sold this fall. I plan to make more over winter.

All kinds of things happen here like everywhere except the subject matter is different. Weather talk consumes conversations. They say a cycle of intense hurricanes will be coming over in the next decade, warm seas around Africa or something seems to trigger them. I'll take it as it comes, evacuate if they tell me to, hold my breath like everyone else.

Inlets and outlets are another big topic. Everything about life out here seems to hinge on how they shift and shoal. Conservationists and environmentalists and government agencies and commercial interests and everyone else involved argue daily over the shifting sands and how to keep this from interrupting life here. It's complicated, how to keep things rolling smoothly without damaging the natural course of nature. It's the same with the wetlands. Some cheer on shopping malls and housing communities while others argue for marsh hawks and yellow-crowned night herons.

The good thing is I don't worry about any of the politics and tug of war. Probably I should since I live here now. And if someone comes along and tells me I've got to move before the ocean sucks me up then we're out of here without argument. It's people like Anna who have lived here forever who fight the fights and speak their peace in pieces. She thinks all development should stop at least a decade to let the sea and sound reclaim some of their home. In her opinion, everyone is making it just fine with the businesses and rentals already here. Her ideas don't do much for a growing economy, but the reason it's so great out here is the lack of commercialization. Who needs shopping malls in the middle of paradise?

We're flying to Memphis next week for Christmas. Dad paid, so it's hard to turn down. I've tried to talk Anna into going with us, but she said she's spent Christmas here for nearly sixty decades and isn't one to break tradition. I tried to talk Dad into coming here, but he won't budge either. We're staying a couple of weeks and plan to visit Claire, too, since she won't come here either, at least not during December. Maybe I can get them both out here next summer. And you guys, too, if you'll come!

Okay, I've got to go think about what to pack for our trip. Wishing you a happy Christmas and New Year! Wish me luck with a kid on a plane.

Sea love,
Sam and Leeci

March 2003

Hey, strangers! It's been way too long. Get off your duffs and send something!

Christmas was wonderful with Dad. Leeci adores him and he adores her. The two never lost sight of each other. He begged me to move back. I begged him to move here. He promises to come this year. I know if I can get him here he'll fall in love with it. Maybe even with Anna's friend Cass, also her business partner. They co-own several rental houses along Highway 12.

Cass is a bit younger than Anna, closer to my selfish dead mother's age. She's been widowed almost twenty years and says she wouldn't have a single fellow from these parts because she already knows their stories. She swears they all have the same personality, the same drive to fish-fish-fish, the same worn skin and salt-wrinkled eyes. I get it. I'm not interested in hitching up with someone from my old haunts. Another good ol' Southern boy can be my buddy any time but isn't my style with the sweat-stained ball cap, baggy jeans, and sloppy sneakers. I know they're not all like that, but it seems like the most popular look these days, a far cry from the chic men's fashions from the '80s (vintage Tommy Hilfiger, please come back!). I think my guy will be more worldly, like Jan Gaynes from Australia but not Jan Gaynes from Australia.

I hope spring is springing where you are. I hope you are in love with something or someone or at least with yourself (but not in an egotistical way). I am in love with the sea. Like Cousteau mused, it truly does cast a spell that draws you in forever.

All the lighthouses here are part of the same spell. The taller ones are coastal lights warning of sandbars. Others are harbor lights to guide boats in. They're beautiful, and I'm pretty sure every one of them along this stretch of North America is haunted. They eek of haunts. Not necessarily evil haunts but haunts all the same.

I'm ready for fish watching. When the season is in full swing, people head to the Hatteras marinas late afternoon to watch the charter boats come in with their ocean loot: tuna, wahoo, mackerel. It's like a competition every day to see who brings in the best catch. Boats flying a blue and white billfish flag upside down are announcing they release white marlin and sailfish. It's a conservation measure. Some boats bring them in anyway and throw them up on the walkways for everyone to gawk at.

Fishing affects me the same as zoos. I'm interested and sad at the same time. It's an ongoing conflict, but I might try to learn surf fishing. There was a workshop in the fall that I missed. The flier is still on my fridge promising to teach fish identification, knot tying, rig prep, tackle selection, and cast netting for bait. Isn't it weird I know a little of what all that means? They also teach you how to read the beach. Let's be clear. You don't cast out just anywhere along the shore. You have to study it for the best spots or you're downright wasting your time.

My beautiful girl gets her first ferry ride to Ocracoke on her birthday. Can you believe she'll be two in a few months? She's going to love how the gulls chase behind the ferry like a huge choir squawking for a treat. It's spectacular.

Add claudication to your list, Richard. It's some sort of muscle pain Anna has in her legs.

Okay, enough about my life. Plus, I need to print this out and get off Anna's computer. Please be in touch soon.

Much love,
Sam and Leeci

May 2003

My extremely estranged friends, it's clear I'm writing to myself these days. And it's lonely, to say the least. Have you abandoned me? Is this payback? My Leeci is starting to wonder if I've made you up, if you are just imaginary friends. What has happened that you're ganging up on me like this?

Pete, you may have become a household name in New York City but not out here, although I did run across an old copy of *The New Yorker* with a write-up about your fellowship award and the show at Copper Bull. We were at The Hut for breakfast. I was digging around in an old stack of mags and newspapers craving some worldly scoop and was so shocked to come across it I spilled coffee on Leeci's coloring book. I tore out the article and put it with our letters, which I keep in a hat box Dad gave me. He said it belonged to his mother, one of the grandmothers I never met, Granddaddy Sam's wife, Ellen, who died the minute Dad was born. I wish I had the original hat that came with the box, or any of her hats or any keepsakes from them or my mom's parents, who died in a car wreck the year before I was born. I wish the article had your picture.

Okay, this is making me sad, sadder than I already am not hearing from you guys. Would you both please send a note saying at least Hello This Is The Famous Pete Wren Alive And Well In New York City and Hello This Is Richard Mabry Alive And Well In Doras, California? Please!

Missing you terribly,
Sam and Leeci

June 2003

Hello This Is The Famous Pete Wren Alive And Well
In New York City.

Yours Truly,
Pete Wren
Famous Painter
Alive And Well In New York City

June 2003

Sam and Richard,

Sorry for that last note and being snarky yet again. I'm worn out, so writing has been the last thing on my agenda. It seems I run around more now than I paint, but the money's been great. I sold every piece in the *Without Warning* series. One woman bought three of them. I can't believe people have the money they have to spend. With a wrist flip, they dole out thousands and thousands more. I wonder how many of them truly appreciate my art or even like it. Seems they're more about collecting for collecting's sake. It gives them some heightened status in posh circles.

Julz has been coming around a bit. Her gallery is on a streak. I'm doing a couple of pieces for a collaboration show there with smaller, less pricey art from about thirty artists. She's smart, that Julz. She's even volunteered to help with an exchange student program. She's taking in some kid from Paris. She's not supposed to pay him but will anyway if he helps with sales.

Richard, add suffocation to your list. And what's the story in Doras?

I could go on with daily details, but they're too dull. To break the monotony, here's something obscure, one of my senseless musings.

Pete, the suffocating closet poet

obsCUREed
by Pete Wren

she comes alone
almost every day
flowing in lovely, elegant clothes

keeping me at bay
breathless almost

chiffon plays the sleeves of her blouse
silk slacks, steel blue
ah, the legs they must house
long, slender, with soft round knees

"Black, no sugar, if you please"
I say to the waiter
who is staring just as me

"Lovely girl" he whispers admiringly
and gasps when she crosses her legs

velvet shoes
with shiny pegs
brass round her wrists
gold rings in her ear

"Lovely girl" I whisper to no one here
and reserve my seat for the day to come

for I a clodden bum
with gold in my teeth
and a brass spittoon
sit here my every noon
sit here in this place
yet to see her face

July 2003

So great to hear from you, Pete. Your poem made me smile. Chiffon plays the sleeves of her blouse? Beautiful!

Have you guys seen the news about Memphis? Dad says they're calling it Hurricane Elvis. It wasn't a hurricane, obviously, but 100 mph straight-line winds are as bad as a Category 2, maybe even a Cat 3.

The old forest tree in his backyard fell and completely crunched the garage and clipped the back side of his neighbor's house. I used to have a tire swing on that old tree. It makes me cringe to think of it falling just twenty feet over, right where his kitchen is. He was pouring a cup of coffee when the storm hit. He said the whole city is devastated.

It's crazy I live out here in hurricane alley, then my hometown hours and hours inland gets slammed with a hurricane-like storm that wipes it out. I want to go and help, but Dad said it's too dangerous, especially for Leeci, and doubts I could even get to him. There's no word yet on when he'll get his power back, and it's sweltering there, so it makes no sense to go. We would be in the way.

On a more cheerful note, summer is still in full swing here, and Leeci just turned two! She goes to a sweet little playschool a couple days a week and may start going three days in September. She's happy as a clam.

I've changed jobs. Imagine that! I liked the restaurant, but the hours are too hard on single motherhood. I needed a day job, so I've become the assistant manager at a bookstore here. It's a bookstore/antique shop mix. I love it!

So, everything is wonderful except worry about Dad and no word from Richard for too long. What gives, Richardnation? I'm not writing another word until we hear from you.

Love,
Sam

September 2003

Sam, please report back immediately that you girls are okay! We must agree on email and phone calls! I've worried to pieces watching the news and weather. I'm not even sure you'll get this.

Did you evacuate? Are you back home? If Gustav was terrifying, I can't even imagine what it was like when Isabel hit. I'm lighting a candle every single night until we hear back that you're all safe and sound. Write immediately please!

I'm sorry I've been absent. I have a great deal to share, but this is not the time.

Literally worried to pieces,
Richard

October 2003

My dear Richard and Pete,

Yes, we are all okay, but Isabel destroyed Anna's house, our sweet little home, mostly with flooding. Amazingly, and I do mean amazingly, *Three Guesses* was not damaged. We managed to get it early last week, plus some clothes and kitchen stuff and my hat box with our letters. I was so afraid they were ruined. All the furniture is definitely ruined. We're in a rental in Manteo and may be for a while. Our mail is being rerouted here temporarily, so use this address until further notice. I can't believe I got your letter, Richard, with everything so upside down here.

We came to Manteo right before Isabel hit. I don't think Anna would have come if not for Leeci. She's such a diehard, but my daughter is like her granddaughter now, more family in the making. She wanted us to be safe somewhere together. And she told me she had a bad feeling, a really bad feeling, so thank goodness for following instincts. Leeci is too little to understand any of this, which is good. She thinks we're on vacation.

It's been total chaos. So much is completely destroyed or totally gone, including one of Anna and Cass's rentals. All their other ones have water and wind damage. The bookstore wasn't hit, so at least I won't have to find a new job, but I'm not sure when we'll reopen.

It's going to be a tough time around here for a long time, and that's all I can say or I'll start crying again. And yeah, since I know you'll ask, this definitely puts some doubt on staying here. I keep thinking I've got life figured out then, no, it has different plans. We'll see.

Richard, please share soon what's going on with you. I'm this close (imagine my finger and thumb smushed together) to sending you both my email and phone, but we all have to agree!!!

Love you guys!
Sam

December 2003

Dearest Sam and Pete,

Have you ever felt as though the world has picked you up and set you back down on grounds unrecognizable? As if you belong nowhere? As if you don't exist? As if people could walk right through you, yet still you feel solid and weighted?

Invisible hands jerked me out of real life for a while. I thought perhaps I'd gone totally lulu in Phoenix, like a dead man among the living. Lost in time immeasurable, I sprawled out on the floors of those lonely, empty rooms and stared bug-eyed at ceiling fans going around and around endlessly. And if I felt like describing to you all the wild visions that passed through my brain, you would be so careful rounding the next big curve hanging over cliffs clutching the ocean.

As if this isn't sad enough, Mother died the same day I set out for Doras. So, here I am without her. My heart is broken. Elsa, her best friend next door, found her in the rocking chair with a cigar hanging out of her mouth. Only Mother would die in such Hitchcock fashion. The way Elsa told it, you'd think she had one of those giant Cuban things stuck in her lips, but I'm sure it was one of those skinny things with a filter. Her two vices: smoking sweet cigars and stealing plants. Her death sentence: heart failure.

Mother's house was the same as always, outfitted with the cheapest furnishings, mostly used. Plastic chairs and cheap throw rugs and lamps that look more appropriate in a sleazy hotel, decades-old decor on the walls like punch rug hangings, ugly ceramic figurines all over the house, bath towels so thin you could read through them, grocery store collector plates and glasses, stacks of mismatched silverware. I grew up in this chaos and realized after moving away that I'd lived in a perpetual thrift store.

Here's the odd part. In the attic, which is huge and spans the whole of the house, are oak and cherry dressers and chests full of things I've yet to discover. Queen Anne chairs and a gorgeous velour chaise lounge and other pieces with names I don't know, hats and scarves and suits, two wedding dresses bright and creamy with pearls and sequins still shiny. There are boxes of shoes and boots and books, old letters and receipts, small chests full of jewelry (matching sets with bejeweled rings and earrings and outrageous brooches), old clocks, framed portraits, on and on.

Growing up, the last thing I ever had on my mind was dawdling about in the attic. I never cared a thing for our house and therefore never explored it. I can't believe all these beautiful heirlooms have been sitting up there all these years, and Mother had no interest, and I had no knowledge of them. This trip down history lane was right above my dense head the whole time.

Bit by bit, I'm clearing out fodder and bringing

down treasures. All the neighbors are bemused except Elsa. Her family and my family have histories arm in arm, and she's been sure to fill me in on extraordinary pieces of it. There's no way I can go into all the stories right now.

Picked up and re-placed. Couldn't have been more perfect timing. But I do miss Mother. I miss her terribly. I wish I'd spent more time with her over the last few years. I wish I'd pushed her to tell me who my father is and what happened to him. Elsa claims to have no clue. I'm not sure I want to know. I'm not sure I've ever even brought him up to you before. Have I?

It looks like I'll be here a while. Mother had a substantial financial portfolio, plus I've managed to save quite a whop over the years. I'm going to take it easy for a bit, relieve myself of worry about relationships and careers and all the rush-through-life nonsense that beleaguers the brain. I've been reading books. I've been watching movies. Alas! I've been sleeping like a sloth.

I should have put this at the top, but I'm so grateful to hear you and Leeci are okay, Sam. Please send an update when possible. I can't imagine what it's been like there. Sending you both huge hugs and a donation to help with furniture and anything else you need. Don't you dare not cash this check!

Your recovering-from-sadness friend,
Richard

January 2004

Oh, sweet Richard, I'm so very sad and sorry about your mom. At least you had her a long time. I hope you will share more with us about her. As for your dad, I'm sure that was the first and only time you've ever mentioned him. I can't imagine how hard your holidays were. I can't believe they've already come and gone.

It's weird how our lives circle each other in mood. I guess it could be another button: LIFE IS A MOOD. Just know I've got you all wrapped up in my heart. And thank you more than words for the financial help, especially in the middle of everything you have going on. It was hard to accept, so I used most of it on Leeci's new bed and dresser, clothes, toys, and basics we couldn't recover.

We move back down to Hatteras by ourselves this weekend into a house owned by one of Anna's friends (use new address). I'm sad we won't be living with her anymore but so excited to have a place of our own. We have an awesome view of the sound, like it's our whole backyard. The place is small and way older than others in the area. Anna said it's been empty quite a while. It's pretty musty and super outdated. The screen door looks like something from another century and squeaks just looking at it. The walls are dull and scarred. I've offered to paint as part of my rent. Stop laughing! I'm sure I can figure that out.

We're all still depressed about Anna's home. It's completely gone now, torn down and scooped away. She is working with insurance and all the hullabaloo for all her properties. I've been helping with phone calls and spreadsheets. I'm not sure if she'll rebuild something there or even if she can. She's still sorting out where to live. I hope she will be near us.

So, as you can imagine, our first Christmas out here was somewhat bleak. We did have a real tree, sort of like Charlie Brown's, but maybe that made it even more special. Leeci was lit up with wonder. And I meant to tell you before that I did finally give my beautiful daughter a middle name. She is Leeci Claire Brooks. Isn't that beautiful? Claire is over the moon about it.

The bookstore opened back up Thanksgiving weekend through Christmas so people would have somewhere close by to get presents. It was too far for me to drive down there every day, so the owner Dorothy (a.k.a. Dot) handled it by herself. Even though it was one of the few places open, she said business was super slow, so I'm creating a newsletter to set out anywhere people will let me. It's a happy experiment to regenerate business and drum up new customers, especially with spring break around the corner.

I've got the basic layout finished and now I'm figuring out what books to feature, plus I'll have a few pictures of the antiques. This is all brand new for me and I'm a little nervous but also excited. So is Dot. She gave me her old computer to use and keeps giving me more responsibilities, especially bookkeeping, which I've been able to help with from here. She even bought a color printer for the newsletter idea. Yay! The first one goes out early March. Wish me luck! I'll send you both a copy. It feels like I finally have a "real" job. Amazing, right?

Anyway, enough babbling. I've got to go finish marking things for the movers. Everything we have so far is boxed up and stored on the first floor.

Write soon and be sure to use the new address. Maybe one day it will be a place I own.

Love you both so much!
Sam

March 2004

Hi, guys! Bravo to Leeci and me! We survived the rest of winter here, though barely since we haven't heard a peep from you two in forever.

Over the last couple of months, we've read oodles of books and spent lots of time with Anna (who finally moved back down here), her on again off again beau, Ed, and Cass. I love her name. Sorry, Pete, it's short for Cassandra.

Our newsletter is all over the island! Dot loves it. I love it. The locals love it, and some have asked me about doing one for them or even advertising in ours. I may have a new calling!

On a somber note, there is still so much recovery going on here. The devastation will never be forgotten, and definitely never forgiven for some. It will be years getting this area back to anything close to before, but all the rebuilding is mind-boggling. I have no idea what tourist season will be like this year.

Meanwhile, and I know you are tired of hearing this, the whole of the Outer Banks truly is haunted from tip to tip. Here I was trying to get away from haunts and I've consciously come to a place full of them, a world consumed by them. Maybe that's why I fit in so well. You can hear moans in the wind, sometimes creaking ships on empty waves, cries even beyond the gulls wailing. I half expect to see Leandra's scarf riding on the breeze. If we do move from life to life trying to get it right, and if there are some who get stuck in between the passing from one to another, there are many stuck here. Haunts floating in limbo, the ones who can't find home or won't leave it.

It's time to snuggle up with my sweet Leeci, who is inching closer to three if you can believe that. I don't care if the experts say kids should sleep on their own. I'm her mom, so I'm the expert in this case. It's simply part of our lives. She'll grow out of it soon enough, so I'm relishing all the cuddle time I can get.

We love our little spot out here, and she loves her room. As promised, here's a picture of her showing it off with Anna (on the right) and Cass. Aren't they all stunningly beautiful? Inside and out, I promise you. I'm so lucky!

Write soon, both of you. No more slacking! Busy times are ahead here.

Love you more than words,
Sam

April 2004

Hello again! I found this today and had to share. May we all hit upon a place to which we mysteriously feel we belong. Perhaps I have found mine along these ancient barrier islands.

Love you!
Sam

From *The Moon and Sixpence*
by W. Somerset Maugham, 1919

I have an idea that some men are born out of their due place. Accident has cast them amid certain surroundings, but they have always a nostalgia for a home they know not. They are strangers at their birthplace, and the leafy lanes they have known from childhood or the populous streets in which they have played remain but a place of passage. They may spend their whole lives aliens among their kindred and remain aloof among the only scenes they have ever known. Perhaps it is this sense of strangeness that sends men far and wide in the search for something permanent, to which they may attach themselves. Perhaps some deep-rooted atavism urges the wanderer back to lands which his ancestors left in the dim beginnings of history. Sometimes a man hits upon a place to which he mysteriously feels that he belongs. Here is the home he sought, and he will settle amid scenes that he has never seen before, among men he has never known, as though they were familiar to him from his birth. Here at last he finds rest.

May 2004

Sam, I'm so glad you and Leeci are okay. Richard, I'm
so sorry about your mom. And yeah, I know it's been
forever since I've written. Apologies.

It's sad all three of us have lost our mothers. Mine
always sent us to bed with food. We were supposed to
eat right away then brush our teeth then go right to
sleep. She was quite dramatic about it in hand move-
ments with nothing said out loud. My father managed
to scarf up most of supper before we had our turn,
so we usually crammed this bedtime food down like
starving dogs, scared he would come snatch it all away
from us. He never knew about this ritual. Probably he
would have killed my mom if he ever found out. She
would take away the dishes at some point in the night.
We never heard her. She held quiet in a way I will never
master.

I didn't even remember this until I watched a movie
last night where a young girl kept sneaking food from
the kitchen and cramming it down at bedtime. By the
time it ended, she ran off into the night to get away
from her abusive parents, and I realized my mom was
preparing us for this same thing. Our bellies would be
full if she snuck us off while my dad was sleeping off a
whiskey rage. Colly knew this, I'm sure. She knew more

than she should for a girl so young and didn't share any of it with me. She kept me sheltered, kept me hidden from the horror, or at least most of it. I'm beyond sad to have lost her. My mom too.

What happened there? I have the same family question as Sam. What on earth made me choose that family? And if we did set ourselves up to meet in this lifetime, why? What for? What could any of us have possibly gained from this union? They're all gone. My dad first, thank God, then my sister, then my mom.

Alice's life revolves around her family. Julz talks to her sister all the time and her father lives in her building, so he's like everywhere all the time. Trust me when I say he's never cared much for me. People travel to visit relatives, old classmates, best friends. Do I even have any relatives? I've never had what most would consider a best friend. You guys are the closest I've come, I think. And Julz. Who knows how I manage to hang onto the worn thread that keeps us keeping on in each other's lives.

Maybe I used my long-gone family simply as a passage, but it sure screwed me up along the way. I guess I'm grateful I'm not attached to other people the way some people seem to be. If anybody has the opportunity to pick up and bound out for anywhere unnoticed, wouldn't it be me? Who would care if I never called or came to visit? Who would even know I'd gone? I am completely and wholly unattached to anyone, to anything, to anywhere. Maybe this is why my paintings are so obscure. Maybe nothing can be too clear. Maybe I'm being a big liar because I'm so attached to Julz it scares me more than anything. She would care if I disappeared. Or at least I hope she would. And I'm attached to you guys, even though our relationship is so surreal I can't paint it.

I promise I'm not whining or complaining or bitter or depressed, well maybe a little depressed. In a questioning mode. Pondering. Bouncing all of this off two of the only three people in the world I feel even remotely connected to.

Degradation.
Pete

July 2004

Hello, dear friends! My apologies for the delay in communiqué, but I've been trying to get beyond grief and adjust to this strange new life back in Doras. If we could get past the letter pact and move into this century with the rest of the world, I could have already emailed or called for a real-time experience. Don't you agree, Pete? Sam and I are on board with this. Won't you please agree?

I loved the *Sixpence* bit, Sam. It was perfect. Bravo for you with the newsletter! You do have talent there. It's fun and professional at the same time. Thanks for sharing it with us.

It's amazing how daily details can strip the wax right off your wings, debilitate your flight, strike you down. I've had to hire a crew to get everything down from the attic because I became immobilized. A family of three burly guys and two sturdy gals have come to my aid. You simply wouldn't believe it. I can no longer walk gracefully through the house. There's barely a path through it all. My lifesavers, the Barbers, are also helping me categorize everything to keep, sell, or giveth away. The first of these is the smallest collection. I learned to love air and space during those dark nights of the soul in Phoenix, plus the Queen Anne look isn't my style.

I've been to five antique stores in the surrounding fifty miles trying to find takers. But alas, they are the thrift stores of my youth, and every owner has the same story. No one in these parts is going to drop a few grand on a vintage armoire that came over from England on a ship. Some 'sort of' friends are having a family reunion next weekend, and one of the visiting nephews is an interior designer. Yes, another nephew. I'm desperate for him to help me figure out what to do.

Like in childhood, I don't blend well with the scenery here. My pink and purple paisleys are shockers in restaurants and grocery aisles, go figure. I'm designing buttons in my head at every turn. Seriously, people, this could be a business. Maybe Sam can be our designer.

Regardless, it looks like I am definitely here for a while sorting all of this out, a bigger chore than I ever imagined. I found an old tape recorder and cassettes, so I'm also starting to record Elsa's stories of our ancestors and how they trekked out here together. Most of it sounds textbook, your typical high school history lesson with the hardships of travel, disease, danger. However, there is one large limb on the family tree with a distinct air of mystery I'm inclined to uncover, though I'll have to use my imagination for now. The Prime Directive is to clear the house out. I know you're wondering how I could let all of this go. Believe me, you'd understand if you could see the scope of it.

On a sneaky note, I'm going out plant-picking tonight. Today is Mother's birthday. And since she's not here, though I'm sure she's here in spirit, the full moon will be my guide to the home of Les Wiggins and his plump wife, Sally. Both scowl at me publicly, so they need their due. They have a delicious blend of Julia Child and Gemini roses two streets over begging to be plucked. I have the perfect sunny plot picked out near the back porch. They'll never see their precious roses again.

Elsa's given me tips on Mother's routine. In the designated planting spot, gently work up the grass layer and set it aside. Dig the hole. Go steal the plant. Snip and tuck to disguise it a bit in case someone dares to accuse. Pop it in, fill in the dirt, and lay the original grass layer around it. Looks like it's been there twenty years. Clever, don't you think? Send happy thoughts that the rose bushes will survive this interruptive transplantation. Ha! A new one for the list!

My reward for pulling off this feat in such dreadful heat will be an original 1930s Phoenix-born Tequila Sunrise. The modern California style of this brilliant libation, immortalized in the 1970s by Mick Jagger and Jose Cuervo, is too orange juicy for me. Plus, I prefer the old-fashioned flavor of crème de cassis over grenadine (in other words, blackcurrant liqueur over pomegranate bar syrup). This simple but lovely recipe came from the 200-year-old bartender at Tibbs Ribs down the street. He claims it's the original, though some argue this refreshing cocktail was first crafted in Tijuana and includes both cassis and grenadine syrup. Either way, neither has orange juice. The irony is not lost on me that I discovered this fabulous version after leaving Phoenix and moving back to California. Give it a try and let me know what you think.

Vintage Tequila Sunrise

2 ounces blanco tequila
1 ounce freshly squeezed lime juice
1 ounce crème de cassis
4 to 5 ounces club soda

Add medium-sized crushed ice (not the slushie kind), tequila, lime and cassis to a shaker and give it 15 to 20 good shakes. Pour it into a tall clear glass then gently pour in the soda. Do not stir. Add a straw and sip slowly, poolside if possible. I promise you won't be disappointed.

Happy Birthday to Leeci! You should receive a package next week with a video camera and tapes along with a vintage set of Pooh books. Maybe they will be valuable some day and she can use them to pay for college.

Nothing for you this time, Pete, but I'm sure I'll come up with something the more I discover here.

Sam, please send me two or three fabulous books. I will call with my credit card number when this ridiculous pact is over.

Wish me luck!
Richard

August 2004

I sit and stare at my paintings knowing they do not belong to me. Art does that. It takes up residence with everyone who experiences it, everyone but the artist. My paintings have never belonged to me, not even tiny pieces of them. I'm a lowly vessel for crafty muses.

I'm feeling a bit like Socrates. I've offended all parties. Accused of impiety even though there's no third party or religious obligation to skirt. But like Soc, I've managed to maintain my opinionated self in choppy waters. I ask questions. I answer questions. I'm a bully about my opinion. I want to tell people exactly what I think and mean. I want people to do exactly the same. But there's nothing precise about anything I do or say. I live in abstraction, precision's toughest sibling. I am a complete contradiction in terms.

At least Socrates wasn't that. He was clear about who he was. Prophet. Enemy. Anomaly. He called people out. He embarrassed upstanding people in outstanding places. He asked questions they couldn't answer. He was stubborn, condescending, sarcastic. Even in the minutes before his execution, he babbled out his thoughts. Then he drank up death and passed his soul freely into the unknown. Probably he had a smirk on his face.

I wonder if she was pretty, his young wife, Xanthippe, with her wicked temper. I wonder if she left him breathless in bed? Did he gaze upon her with longing? I gaze at Julz with longing, but now that's all shot. I saw her yesterday loving on her very young exchange student. Is she that desperate?

I am in no mood to write anything more, so here's a poem I wrote when I lived with Alice. I watched it happen.

Happy belated birthday to our beautiful Leeci.

Consternation.
Pete

eDgeS
by Pete Wren

In the window across the yard
they are kissing
and more
so I have to look away
for just a moment
then back
and they're gone.

I wake at two and look again.
He's standing at the window looking back
not at me but at moon shadows on the lawn
and the cat resting at the edge of the face the oak makes.

I wake at four and look again
She's standing at the window looking back
not at me but at her hands against the dark
and the lines resting at the edge of the curve the night
makes.

I wake at six and look again.
The cat is looking back
not at me but at the day coming to be
and his tail resting at the edge of the seat the window
makes.

September 2004

Hey, guys! Sorry it's been a bit.

Do you think we can fly? I do. I think we can lift right off this earth and plow right up to the clouds. This was snuffed out of us at some point. I watch Leeci on the shore with her arms flapping like a bird, stretched out trying to catch a ride on the breeze. She wants desperately to fly. So do I. I believe we were meant to fly, born to fly but tethered by doubt.

Richard, I've already filled the video tapes with everything Leeci—pretending to fly, running along the shore chasing sand pipers, building shell towers, sleeping. You are such a giver, and words fail to express how grateful and thankful I am. I sure hope I can give you something special someday.

I'm like you, Pete. I haven't felt much like writing, especially with all the weather events we've already had here or nearby. Everyone is worn out with storms and flooding and crazy intense winds, one thing right after another. But we're still here. I still love it here. I want to be able to follow in Anna's footsteps and live here forever, be another local fixture like a patch of ice at the edge of the sound in December. I have no inclination to roam.

Dad came out this summer and fell in love with the

Outer Banks, especially Ocracoke. I think I'm close to convincing him to come back for Christmas this year, maybe for all of December even though it's not the best time for a visit. It depends on the weather. Everything does! I still want him to fall in love with Cass. She was visiting her daughter in Baltimore when he was here, so they didn't get to meet. Of course, I have no idea what kind of woman (or person) Dad might be interested in. No idea at all.

It's kind of hard to imagine older people falling in love. Well, I guess I shouldn't say that since I don't know how old you guys are. Older than me it seems, like big brothers. Richard, I'd say you're the oldest, then Pete, then me. And Pete, I loved the poem you sent. I love your writing. You're such a romantic!

Am I ever going to fall in love? I've been reading about love languages, which sounds so totally hippie, doesn't it? Maybe I'm in the wrong era. Anyway, we're all supposed to have one primary and one secondary. I'm not nearly that simple, more like a bundle of three. I need 1) words of affirmation, 2) quality time, and 3) touch. Gifts I love but don't need. Acts of devotion, well, that depends. Probably the best thing is to have a good balance of all five.

Pete, you and Julz have your own love language. You've got to find it, bring it to the surface. Can't you tell her? Tell her you love her. She gets you, right? Haven't you said that? Maybe you misread what you saw with the student. Have you asked her about it? When was the last time you were together? I know it's none of my business, and obviously I don't expect answers, but I wish you two would get together for good and get past the past. I don't know who proposed the idea that you love someone because they sing a song that only you can hear, but it's certainly fitting here. I think Julz hears your song and you hear hers.

Write soon! Love and kisses from Leeci.

Sam

September 2004

Pete, I must say I agree with Sam's Pete-loves-Julz initiative. Come on, don't ruin this. Love her. Let her love
you. Get away together. Get out of New York for a
spell. Come here if you'd like. I'm over this old agreement. Why are we keeping this up?

Speaking of love, I'm in it! Remember the family
reunion? I immediately fell in love with the interior designer nephew Carlton, who I wish was on my side but
unfortunately runs in a different lane. I'm in love with
him anyway because he's completely solved the problem of how to sell off these treasures. We're having
an auction in a few weeks. Carlton knows people who
know people who know people who have people, and
all of them are making a trip to Doras for the big day
because no one in Doras or the surrounding hundred
miles gives a flip about any of it. I have no idea where
he plans to put these people up. They'll come on Friday
to preview, then bidding begins Saturday morning. It's
like my own personal harvest. Mother is so here too.

I've engaged the Barbers again. They're like a one-
stop shop. They'll pack everything for shipping, keep
track of where things are going, schedule deliveries.
Carlton has it all worked out with them. I haven't the
slightest idea about those details nor do I care to know.

All I know is what I'm paying everyone to clear this all out. Carlton believes I'll make a hefty five-figure profit. Can you feel the beam coming off my cheeks? Though I do think he's thinking a little high.

Maybe I'll sell the house afterward and move on. Mother doesn't mind. She can go with me anywhere now. But I might keep it. Refurbish the whole thing and blow out the back with a deck and a hot tub. Who knows. I'm not attached to it. It certainly isn't attached to me. No one here except Elsa is attached to me. There isn't anyone else here for me to love. Literally no one. All I have is the collection of things I'm taking with me when I do jump ship.

Sam, yes, we are meant to fly! Encourage our dear girl to keep trying. One day she'll lift right up and wave to us from above. Maybe then we can cast aside our doubts and find the courage to join her in the clouds.

And now to the hats. These are early Christmas presents. I hope they fit. They're treasures from the attic, so the head measurements you never sent for the other hats I never sent would be no good anyway. I've had them cleaned and specially packaged for storage in case you don't want to wear them, though I do hope you will. They're very old, and I'm sure they have stories to tell.

Pete gets a steel gray Fedora, Sam a cobalt Tam, Leeci a gold beret.

Syncopation!
Richard

PS: Sam, I'm terrified to watch the news anymore. East coast weather makes my blood pressure soar. Hurricanes! Tropical Storms! Tropical Depressions! I'm praying for all of you every day now. And I don't even pray!

October 2004

Hello from the Outer Banks! We love our hats, Rich-ard! Thank you! We wear them every day. The beret fits perfectly on Leeci's crazy thick curls. I made a hanger out of an old piece of wood and two glass drawer pulls and hung it by the screen door, so that's where they live when not on our heads. Leeci glued a star on it and beamed like she'd just created a history-making work of art.

She asks when you are coming to visit her. She doesn't know we still have the mail-only pact holding us back, which is beyond outdated at this point. I agree wholeheartedly, Richard. Why are we keeping this up? It's been what, a hundred years now since we started this? Since last century! The world is leaving us behind, you old fogies. Come see us! I'm great with email and phone calls in the interim. Pete, again, you must also agree.

The house Anna and Cass keep off the market for friends and family had the least damage from Isabel and was fixed quickly, so let's plan something ASAP for this spring so we can get it on their calendar before someone else does. Please!!!

We are okay weather-wise, at least for now. I swear we'll try not to talk about it if you ever get here, but people do literally talk endlessly about it, the history of storms and all the predictions of the next season and the thousand after that. They talk about past hurricanes like relatives: Connie, Emily, Gloria. Remember this happened and that happened. It goes on and on. The more current ones, like wicked Isabel, are still such open wounds they aren't brought up casually like old ancestors. They remain difficult everyday conversations because the destruction is still part of everyday life.

Okay, enough about the terrors of weather. I'm off to bunk down for the night. Leeci is spending the night with Anna. Don't I wish I was having a sleepover?

Oh, I almost forgot. Richard, I made your Vintage Tequila Sunrise way back when for Anna and me, sound-side though instead of poolside. Delicious! Anna said it's like sipping on spiked candy.

Love you guys,
Sam

November 2004

Happy Holidays, dearest friends! I know it's not your thing, Pete, but I wish you the merriest of merriment all the same.

I'm preparing to settle in for a long winter's stay here in Doras. Everything I didn't want is gone. While I did not make five figures from the auction, the total came close and has been added to my nest egg. The house is a bit stark now with just a few lovely pieces I decided to keep. I'm bundled up cozy in the back den with several boxes and stacks of history to dawdle in over the next few months. For once, my research leads me down the road of family Mabrys and Carsons and even Brontës if you can believe it. It's possible I'm a bit of British bloke after all with relatives hailing from Yorkshire. I hope to find the truth of my ancestry in all these piles.

Speaking of truth, Sam, it's time I reveal something that may seem terribly intrusive. I truly hope not, but I've kept this in so long I'm about to burst. My hands are shaking as I type.

I have a statement to make and a question to ask. You totally call the shots. I will abide by whichever answer you give, yes or no.

The statement: I found your Australian Jan Gaynes.

The question: Do you want to know about him?

My apologies for the abruptness. If I could talk to you on the phone, you would hear the worry in my voice that I've crossed a personal line far from my business. I don't want to upset you, but I did want to see what I could find out about your mystery lover, more importantly your daughter's father, especially since I too grew up without one. I consider Leeci my niece, as you are my adopted family now, so I thought it pertinent to find out if this person still exists, what he does, where he lives. I will say right off that I've found no bad news and hope that helps settle your mind. He appears to be a legitimate and more than decent chap.

Again, this is your choice. We'll close the book immediately if you are not interested. And please know this inquiry was done purely from love, not idle curiosity. I desperately hope you are not upset with me.

Speaking of love, Pete, have you told Julz yet how much you love her?

I'm on the edge of my seat for us all.

Much love,
Richard

November 2004

Richard, I was immediately upset with you then immediately not upset then upset again then not. Now I'm in between.

Yes, I want to know about Jan Gaynes. You have no idea how many times I've thought about trying to find him. Since you say there isn't bad news, at least that you know of, I think I can take it. I have no idea what I'll do with it. But curiosity has been killing this cat too!

I can't tell you guys how many dreams I've had about him, series-like daydreams that play out like stories. I imagine waking up with him beside me. I see him and Leeci building sandcastles. I see him around the card table with my friends. I have visions of us buying a house together, grilling out in the backyard, even having another kid!

Pete, you must weigh in here. This affects our precious Leeci and might affect us all since it could totally change my life.

I'm all over the place right now. I won't sleep at all tonight, I'm sure.

Truly overwhelmed,
Sam

December 2004

My dear Sam, I'm sorry to overwhelm you but so relieved to tell you about Jan. I hoped to hear from Pete by now, but alas, still no word. Why have you abandoned us, old friend? This is a legitimate question requiring a legitimate answer. I know we've all disappeared at times, but it's important we hear from you immediately about all of this.

I gathered this info months ago but never could find the right moment to share until we got your letter about hippie love languages. I could literally feel your loneliness for a mate. Then when you wished you were having a sleepover (and we know exactly what kind you meant), it felt like the perfect time to come clean.

I'm going to share only some of Jan's life details, not everything I've found, because I don't want to reveal too much in case you decide to seek him out. People are supposed to find out about each other from each other. So, forgive me for stating basic facts without my usual novelesque prose. Well, I may throw in a little. There are some remarkable coincidences.

First, his full name is Jan Lee Gaynes. Neither Jan nor Lee are chopped from longer names. What a brilliant happenstance! To me, it was the first sign to keep digging, at least for Leeci.

Second, he lives at this very moment in New Bern, North Carolina. I'm still getting my breath on this one. Of all the joints in all the world, he lives just a few hours from yours. Get a map. Look it up. You're not oceans and continents apart, only a sound away. He can be on the Cedar Island Ferry to Ocracoke in less than two hours then directly to you from there, or vice versa for you from Hatteras.

Third, he wrote the enclosed book of poems expressing his love for sea and sound. Wildly implausible connections, I say! I procured copies for us all by contacting his office.

As for his history, Jan was born in America, his mother's country, then moved with his family to Australia, his father's country, stayed through university at Melbourne then moved back over here and received his PhD at Duke. He is a highly respected, sought out (and unmarried) environmental engineer and hydrologist. He has led numerous projects to solve the ever-growing threats of pollution to the Albemarle-Pamlico watershed, basically your entire area, caused by an ever-growing human population whose life and food needs disrupt the natural balance of nutrients in the water for the collective of these humans, plus all the plants and animals and sea and sound life. It's spelled out more eloquently in the brochure from his consulting company I've tucked in your books. His picture is on the back of the brochure. Leeci looks just like him.

There you have it. An inch-thick folder's worth of details brought to you in great brevity.

His poems are lovely. My favorite is *Carry Me*, page 11. The first two lines: Carry me softly restless wind/ Let me calm your hurried pace. Isn't that beautiful?

Sam, I'm anxious to know what's going on in your mind, and you can call right now if you wish. Without permission or agreement, I've enclosed my card. You, too, Pete. Call right now and I'll set up a three-way conversation no matter the time, day or night or in between.

Sea love extraordinaire!
Richard

December 2004

Dear Richard and Pete (wherever you are),

I don't know what to say. I don't know how to feel. I'm freaked out Jan Gaynes is so close to us. And I cannot believe his middle name is Lee! I mean seriously? It does feel like a sign. Leeci definitely has his eyes. I'm sure I wear the pulse of our stormy afternoon on my face every time I look at my beautiful girl.

I really do not know what to do with this. I've been out of my mind thinking about him. I'm inclined to go spy on him immediately. I'm just as inclined to tuck this information away forever and never think of it again. I'm perplexed. I'm still a bit perturbed. But I'm also grateful. See what a mess I am! I want to call, but Pete has still not agreed. Pete, please!!!

Winter is a tough life in these parts, especially the mulling time like now in the wee hours. Leeci fell asleep on the couch, and I can't bear to move her. I'm thinking of beautiful Jan Lee Gaynes, thinking of magic, thinking of souls and pondering if we are soulmate three-somes (me and you guys, me and Leeci and Jan), and all of this is getting us closer to somewhere together.

Three Guesses is in the perfect place now. I've moved it a few times trying to find the right spot. It hangs over an old desk by the screen door. I found the desk in

Anna's storage unit. Her aunt gave it to her when she turned thirteen, so it's definitely got some age on it. Anna said she promptly painted the dreary dark wood a bright green, which is peeling off now. I love it. It's totally bohemian like me.

The back porch light from my closest neighbor gives *Three Guesses* an entirely different life than regular daylight or lamplight. It plays with all the textures. You do have to look at it from far away to see a shape in the swooshes. And since you painted it, Pete, I'm sure it is a woman. She seems to be walking along water, walking along a shoreline shrouded by a dusty mist. Maybe the darker areas on either side are sea and sound?

Could this be the twin of *Wondering Ju*? I think Richard asked before. Do you have a picture of it so we can compare? Does Julz? Maybe it's Leeci in a past life, all grown up and walking along the seashore while sorting out her plans to come back to this time to be with us.

I know we're not supposed to care so much what it's about, but the name itself begs us to ponder. I'll stop trying to guess and won't care to ever know if you'll please send us a note, even a postcard with the Pete Wren Is Alive and Well in New York City bit. It's been too long. We need to know you're okay. And I'm desperate to know what you're thinking about Jan Gaynes. I want you to agree to phone calls at least so we can talk in person. I'm feeling sad to think you've dropped us. I don't think I could take that. Especially not now with this at my feet.

Richard, thank you, I think. So many thoughts are slamming me all at once, and I can't organize a single one of them rationally. I'm going to talk to Anna and Claire and see what they think I should do.

Sending love in color and confusion,
Sam

January 2005

Pete Wren, are we ever going to hear from you again? Are you upset with me for finding Jan Gaynes? I know you are big-time famous and all, but please don't forget your small-time pen pals. We need you!

Sam, enclosed is a pendant for Leeci, a miniature of *Three Guesses* made from the photo I sent Pete moons ago. I'm surprised how well it turned out. I hope she loves it. Meanwhile, what do Anna and Claire have to say about Jan Gaynes?

I have all sorts of things to share about my family research. It's intoxicating and carries me through stories that sound like movies. I'm putting a book together, so you'll have to wait for the full lowdown. It will likely be a self-published venture more for my benefit than anyone else's. Well, Elsa might enjoy it since it includes some of her family history.

History is such a mystery. How odd yesterday is now history. This morning is now history. We think of it on a grand scale, years and decades and eras, but history spirals out second by second, hour by hour. It's always almost tomorrow, which soon becomes yesterday, ancestor of today.

The history of how people are connected is equally riveting and dull. My connection to the Brontës is slippery loose and more down an Irish trail than British. My familial connections elsewhere are typical, but how some of them came to be is a bit spellbinding. I'm having a harder time piecing it all together than I expected. In some cases, I'm up to box tops with documentation. In others, vague portions are broken and without strong chronological hints.

In a series of letters I found between a couple I've yet to identify, the dates are written at the top right of every letter but with only the month and day. For our letters, not including the day will probably never matter historically. For their letters, excluding the year matters a great deal!

They talk of a war. Which one? Where? When? Elsa has no idea about these. So much of the collection is disintegrating. Here is what I can make out from a February 7 letter at some point eras ago. "I believe Father will have to send Lowell away or hide him in some way. He isn't fit to fight. This doesn't deter them. They are taking them all, all our young men, no matter their age or disability. It is a dreadful time. I pray daily that you remain safe. My heart is with you always. My love is ever strong and faithful." The signature is only a fancy L.

Did he survive? Did he come back from that war with her letters, or did her letters come back without him? Or were they sent to a relative, not a lover, maybe a cousin or a sister. Maddening!

If I took the time to write down my past, it would be the dullest of dull, nothing intriguing except our mysterious pen pal connection. I need to add some verve to this boring old life. I can assure you it won't occur here in Doras. Even my enthusiasm about all this family history is about their lives, not mine. My excitement about Jan Gaynes is Sam's life and Leeci's, not mine. However, as past lives go, I might be him, the one from the war. It's oddly familiar, the writing, the smell of the paper. Imagine that! I literally could be him. And if we do carry the same DNA from life to life, technology will eventually catch up and tell us who we've been. Heady stuff.

I need to get out of here for a while., Maybe I should head to the Outer Banks this spring. Pete, you have to come too. We can't shake up this soulful threesome. It's one for all and all for one all the way, like The Three Musketeers. What do you think? Please write soon. Or call! Or email! Here again is my card. We're both worried to pieces about you.

My love to all,
Richard

January 2005

Please do come here, sweet friends! Leeci and Anna and the Outer Banks want to meet you. Plus, I really need your help with this Jan business. I can't stop thinking about him. I think about him so much I feel I can say his name like that now without saying Jan Gaynes or Jan Lee Gaynes, knowing he's real, more than a mirage in my mind.

Reality finds us eventually, or we find it, though it's never lost. It's always sitting right here beside us, inside us, all around us, waiting to be acknowledged. It feeds our soul, even when it feels like it's stealing from our plates.

I'm constantly searching for the perfect soul food, whatever flavor mirrors my mood. I've been keeping a journal over a year now, ever since I started at the bookstore, to capture nourishing nibbles. One of my favorites from Walt Whitman: "Whatever satisfies the soul is truth."

There are so many by Rumi I could fill my whole journal with his wisdom alone. Here's a fav. "I have been a seeker and I still am, but I stopped asking the books and the stars. I started listening to the teaching of my Soul." Isn't that divine? He also said, "The breeze at dawn has secrets to tell you. Don't go back to sleep." Fran Lebowitz considers life as something we do when we can't sleep.

I've felt more awake in the last few years than I've felt my entire life. The biggest part of that is being a mom, I'm sure, but I still feel deeply asleep in so many ways, even though sleep is a commodity these days with my mind in pure overdrive.

If I could see more clearly, or get a definitive sign from the universe, maybe I wouldn't be so scared to fully wake up, to take that first step to reconnect with Jan. I wish you would tell me exactly what to do and not do, what to say and not say. Anna and Claire won't, of course, but they've more than hinted that I should grab this opportunity like my life depends on it. And Leeci's, too, of course.

Jan and I created a human being, a precious little girl. We gave her soul a life to live in the here and now. These serious facts make my heart swell up like a balloon.

Did we plan this in another life? Is it right or wrong to bring them together? Is it right or wrong to keep them apart? What will Jan do or not do? What will he say or not say? What if he hardly remembers me? What if he wants to take her away from me? You can imagine why I sleep only in spurts. These repetitive thoughts are an endless stock of exploding grenades. I wish I could take a long walk and clear my head, but it's freezing here. Maybe I'll take a drive and see if that helps.

Richard, the pendant is beautiful. You must know she adores it.

Pete, I appeal to you again and again. Please be in touch. Richard is right. We are worried to pieces. We need to hear from you pronto!

Soul-filled love for you both,
Sam

January 2005

Dear Sam and Richard,

My name is Julie Reese. You know of me as Julz. I'm sorry I haven't contacted you before now. I've waited to write, thinking things would improve. Unfortunately, they have not.

Pete is in a deep depression and has been struggling for months now. He did misinterpret what he saw with me and the French student Farrin, as Sam suspected. Farrin had just learned his grandmother died. She raised him, and here he was thousands of miles away from her. He was crying so hard I wrapped him up in my arms. That's when Pete walked in. He didn't stay long enough for an explanation and wouldn't respond to me no matter how many times I called. I felt the most terrible sense of dread, not only because of that incident, but because his anger was out of control long before then.

I finally went to his loft. It was wrecked. Paint was flung everywhere. Paintings were torn. Some were cut up into hundreds of pieces. I found him curled up in the middle of the bathroom floor. I found your recent letters unopened in a pile by the door and all the others, including printouts of all the ones he sent to you, thrown together in the bottom of his paint closet. I have to say I was quite shocked. He's never said a word about you. I had no idea you existed.

Please don't ever tell Pete I've told you any of this and be sure to destroy this letter. I'm afraid we would lose him forever if he found out I read through your letters and shared his condition with you. No one knows except me and another friend. We've been helping him as best we can and have managed so far to keep this a secret. I don't know what he might do if he thought everyone who adores and abhors him was aware of his current state.

We will have to seek formal treatment if this goes on much longer. Perhaps we should have already, but I want to give him a little more time to shake out of this. In the meantime, please keep including him in your letters. I believe your presence in his life has meant more to him than anything, more than his art, maybe more than me.

Thank you for being his best unmet friends on the planet. I hope to meet someday in person at Pete's side.

Sincerely yours,
Julz

February 2005

Sam, I realize this is super short notice, but please see if the family place is available the first couple of weeks in April. Jan Gaynes is giving a talk in Manteo on April 1st on water purification techniques or something like that. This appears to be an open forum for the common man, and we're going IF you're up for it. I'm on the edge of my seat to book a flight to Norfolk, then I'll grab a car and head down Highway 12 as fast as I can.

Pete, stop being estranged from us. You're our brother now whether you like it or not, so come on back to the family fold and book this trip. If Julz is still in your life, bring her along. You can fly into Norfolk and ride down with me to our darling girls. I am happy to book your flights. Let me know how I can help. I've enclosed my card yet again.

Both of you, we are done with not meeting or talking in person. I'm over it. You are my family, and I love you beyond written words. I want to meet you in person and spend time with you and share stories and laugh like idiots into the wee hours of the morning and maybe even cry a little if we must. I want to get out of this gossipy little town and feel ocean breezes. Sam, I want to see if there is something of Jan Gaynes for you and sweet Leeci. Pete, I want you to paint us or write a poem or a story about us. I want Julz to be a part of this surrogate family because we know you love her, and it's time you bring her directly into your heart and into our lives. Life is too short, so we're crazy to keep on this way.

I repeat: Life is too short. We are wasting precious time with this years-old agreement of only writing letters back and forth and forth and back. It has served us beautifully, and I treasure every one of them, and we may continue to write for the rest of our years, but right now I want more. I need more. I need to know you both beyond ink and once-in-a-while meanderings and sketchy life details. I need to meet my niece!

So there. It's settled. I expect a quick response of YES! Right away. I repeat: Right away!

SEA YOU SOON!

Love to all!
Richard

February 2005

Come hither, brothers! Anna confirmed the friends and family house is open the whole month of April so far. I am 30,000 feet up in the air about meeting you in person and both thrilled and nervous as a cat about seeing Jan. This is something you totally have to walk me through, both of you twisting my arms. Maybe break my legs so you have to wheel me in. Should we take Leeci? I don't know what to do. Again, I will need you both there to do this with me.

Pete, please say you'll come. I'm beyond worried you haven't written for so long. We miss you. Leeci can't wait to meet you. You must come see her before she's all grown up. Her precious little girl years are flying by so fast. I want you to paint her, even if it's abstract.

Love you guys so much I'm bursting wide open!
Sam

February 2005

Dearest Sam and Pete,

I have more details about Jan's event. I was mistaken. It's a three-day weekend affair for engineers, and the open community forum is Monday, April 4th.

It occurs to me I've been a bully about this. Let us step back a few paces. This is completely up to you, Sam. If you decide you want to go, we'll be right there to guide you in and hold you up. If not, we won't go. Right, Pete? You must come to our dear girl's aid. On this I will continue to be a bully.

I fly into Norfolk on Thursday, March 31st. It's a late arrival, so I'll stay there overnight and drive down Friday. See enclosed flight info, and I've included my card. Again.

The first thing I plan to do when I see you girls is grab Leeci up in my arms and twirl her around. Regardless of absent bloodlines, Leeci is our niece, Pete, and you are our brother and Sam is our sister. The chance to see your faces, to breathe your air, brings light to my lonely heart and tears to my tired eyes.

With brotherly (and uncle) love,
Richard

March 2005

Hello, Wonderful People! I can't wait to finally meet in person. You ARE coming, right Pete? I'm picking Richard up Friday morning April 1st, and we'll come back for you whatever day you can get here. I want you to know I did call him so he wouldn't rent a car. I was worried a letter wouldn't make it in time.

There's something I want to tell you both now so I don't end up breaking into pieces during one of our late-night spill-all wine talks. I've told you about my mom. What I probably didn't mention is that I turned twelve the same day. Yep, she checked out on my birthday. What a remarkable date to pick, right? Your daughter's birthday! And not just any birthday but the last one of childhood.

It was a Saturday. I woke up to find a haphazard cake sitting on the kitchen counter and a box of candles spilled out on the floor. There wasn't a sound in the house. Dad's car was gone. She was in bed, so I laid around all day doing nothing. I looked in on her a couple of times. She hadn't moved. I didn't even think about waking her up. I was enjoying the peace and quiet. My parents weren't happy, so our house was usually a buzz of discontent.

Dad got back early afternoon. He had been helping

a friend with his roof. He couldn't believe she was still in bed. Then neither of us could believe she would never get out of bed again, at least not alive. Pills. I don't know what kind, and I don't care.

There's so much more to this story I don't want to relive, so please don't make me when you are here. I'm giving you this much to explain something. Before the stormy day encounter with Jan, I was toying with the idea of checking out myself. My mom's choice didn't seem so awful anymore. Life didn't seem to be my bag. I was so tired of it, or tired of not having one, tired of being alone. Then there was Jan. Then there was Leeci.

You see, Jan Gaynes may have saved my life. That's what makes this so much bigger. That's why I couldn't possibly walk toward him without you by my side. I hope you understand how desperately I need both of you here. And I hope you are okay with me sending my phone and email, Pete, because time is running out!

Sending oodles of love,
Sam

March 2005

To Sam and Richard, my extraordinary friends,

I'm so sorry I disappeared. And I'm terrified to promise I will get to you because what if I can't? But I know I must. But what if I can't get on the plane or even out of this building? See how crazy messed up I am? I have to come, I know. For all of you and for Julz. She's coming with me because I'm a lucky idiot and she is a blue diamond. She booked our flights this morning. We get into Norfolk on Friday. How fitting it will be April Fool's Day.

Even if Julz has to drug and drag me, I'll be there. She is calling you both this afternoon in case this letter doesn't arrive in time. She may be calling you right now, so you already know all of this, but I wanted to write anyway. No email for me.

I am both thrilled and nervous to meet in person. What if you aren't what I expect? What if I'm not what you expect? Though it won't matter, will it? We are who we are. Thank goodness you're driving us, Sam, or I might be even more terrified about this trip. Julz and I are pure city folks. We have no idea how to drive down a coastline.

Again, I'm sorry about going dark. I've been dark a long time, long before we met, which I'm sure you

figured out way back when. I might or might not explain more when we're together. Like with Sam and
her mom, we don't have to relive all the pieces of our
stories.

The world is changing so quickly. Everyone and
everything is changing at light speed so fast it's hard
to keep up. It scares me how fast. I don't see where or
how to fit in it. I definitely can't paint it anymore, to
the point of going crazy. Literally. I do still get a poem
in now and then. Tagged on here is one for Jax and
Jamber.

Congregation.
Pete

CaTnAp
by Pete Wren

I'll fall deep
into sleep
twitch
cause I'll get an itch
about the tom in the yard
staring hard
at the babe on the sill
laying still
thinking about me see
cause I'm bigger than him
that old tom tim
sissy
pissy old guy
with a bad eye
then I'll get up and eat
lick my feet
go pee
and think gee
when the box is clean
as opposed
to its usual scene
then I'll go back to the curl
lay up in a swirl
Max the cool cat
yeah

July 2005

Hello, Pete Wren of New York City and Richard Mabry of Doras, California!

Are you surprised to get snail mail again? Do you realize this all started exactly seven years ago? I know you must be smiling right now to get something besides bills and junk but more than anything to have just opened a happy friend letter. I decided we can't let the old-fashioned way go out of style, not completely, and it seems a fitting way to honor our incredible-beyond-words friendship. The nostalgia, you know. I'm a bit weepy to think our days of sending letters are over.

You may be tired of hearing this since it's how I start every conversation now, but I want to repeat how much I love and appreciate you both and Julz for coming here to help me figure out the whole Jan thing. I couldn't have done it without you.

Richard, I'm literally beside myself that you're thinking of moving here! You know we'll have to get you on some blood pressure medicine or anxiety pills to calm your weather fears. Anna and Cass have three places for you to look at next month. One is near me in Hatteras (my favorite). The other two are seaside in Rodanthe (too far away and kind of lonely looking) and Avon (smaller and quaint but still too far from me).

Cass's crew will be out of the family house early

Sunday. It will be a blast for you to stay here with Leeci and me until it's ready, then maybe we'll come stay with you off and on during your visit if you'll have us. Leeci is ecstatic. I think Crumb is too. I can't believe he's still around. If you do end up moving here, we'll have to figure out how he and Jax can be friends. And hopefully you and Jan will be friends too. Maybe-maybe-maybe, if he doesn't flee from me.

Pete, I'm beyond excited you're coming back this fall! You're going to love Anna's newest place on Ocracoke. I know you're already madly in love with the island, but seriously you might never want to leave (well, maybe in the dead of winter and certainly during a hurricane). It might be your forever scene to squeeze sand in your hands. Please see if Julz will come. I want more time with her. She is definitely a gem.

Tonight's sunset is a mesmerizing mix of them with swirls of garnet, carnelian, and amethyst filling the sky. I'm basking in the beauty of it all alone this evening, but I don't mind. Leeci is with Anna because…drum-roll please…Jan is coming tomorrow for the weekend!

I wanted to send an email to tell you, but I was afraid you would call or email back with a ton of questions, and I don't want to talk about it and possibly jinx anything. By the time you get this, Jan's visit will be old news, and I'm sure I'll set up a call with you the minute he leaves. (Love the three-way calls, Richard!) I wonder… Was I giddy or grumpy? Giddy, I hope.

I'm sorry I've been so vague about my conversations with him but haven't wanted to share much yet. I'm still in shock he recognized me, that he wanted to reconnect. My God, his eyes melt me, even from the brochure picture. His voice mesmerizes me. I don't want to get off the phone. I think he feels the same way. We dawdle over tiny daily details to keep from hanging up.

I haven't said a word about Leeci, who just turned four! I need real time with him before I come clean and tell him this whole thing was not mere coincidence. It's been crazy hard not to spill it. I hope with all my heart that he understands my hesitation. I hope it doesn't ruin everything when I finally do tell him, but I need to know more about him before I throw the truth on the table, before I introduce him and my precious girl. For both their sakes, this has to happen soon. It will be shockingly obvious to him she's his.

Since I haven't shared much about our calls, I'll share a little secret to end my rambling rhetoric. I've been writing a slew of songs. A lot of them are sad sappy things, but this one is a sultry, sexy number, a bit country and definitely soulful. Claire pushed me to submit it to the U.S. Copyright Office, so I did! Can you believe that? It's legit registered. Here's the opening, and when we're together again I'll serenade you with the whole wonderful thing. I'm not a great singer, so no judgment, got it!

Are you thinking 'bout me?
Are you thinking 'bout being with me?
Are you thinking 'bout holding me?
What do you see?

Now lay your cards on the table, man.
No, I'm not looking for a plan.
Just wanna know where your heart is at.
Are you thinking 'bout me?

'Cause I've been thinking 'bout you.
I've been thinking 'bout being with you.
I've been thinking 'bout holding you.
That's what I see.

To answer the question you're asking right now, yes!
Yes, you can go with me to the Grammys to accept my
gilded gramophone for Songwriter of the Year.

And here's one more big-big secret I can't believe
I've kept all these years. I almost got fired over *Three
Guesses*. It was never supposed to go to Phoenix. It was
probably never going to get out of storage because it
was hidden behind a giant mirror no one wanted, and it
wasn't even recorded properly in the database! I found
it by accident and sent it on purpose. I'll tell you all
about it someday.

Enough about secrets and back to current reality. I

sit here with change on the horizon again, so I'm going to kick back and enjoy the rest of this glorious evening and soak up these precious moments before it comes my way. I have no idea what happens from here. I get three guesses, right?

As for you guys, Pooh nailed it: I knew when I met you an adventure was going to happen.

Love you so much, and I'm over the moon in love with our grown-up pen-pal adventure turned into family. Aren't we the luckiest people in the world?!?

Yours forever,
Sam

Acknowledgments

My immense love and gratitude go to my amazing parents, Gerald and Joyce McClain, for a lifetime of encouragement, and to family, friends, and colleagues who have cheered me on throughout my writing life and this exciting journey.

Many thanks to the amazing Regal House Publishing duo, Jaynie Royal and Pam Van Dyk, for loving this story and selecting it as the winner of the 2023 Fugere Book Prize, to the RHP team for bringing it to life, and to many fellow authors for sharing their time and wisdom.

And thank you Sam, Richard, and Pete for sharing your messy, marvelous lives with us.